'You and me, Caroline.'

'You and me?'

He stayed silent for a moment, straightened carefully from leaning on the bench, watching her. 'Have I been reading you wrongly all this time, then?' he finally said. 'Are you interested, Caroline?'

'Yes!' she answered wildly. 'Of course I am. You know I am. Isn't that why you backed off for the last six weeks? You knew how I felt.'

'Six weeks isn't long.'

'Do you want longer?' she offered, hardly knowing what she'd said. 'Because if—'

'No. I do not want longer.' He reached for her and wrapped his arms around her waist, looking down into her face with eyes like the sun on the sea. 'I do not want one second longer, Caroline.'

Medical Romance™
is proud to present another emotionally
gripping duet by talented author

Lilian Darcy

Caroline and Nell work at

GLENFALLON HOSPITAL.

Glenfallon is a large rural community
in the beautiful wine-making region of
New South Wales, Australia

THE DOCTOR'S UNEXPECTED FAMILY
is Caroline's story.

Read Nell's story,
THE A&E CONSULTANT'S SECRET,
the second book in this stunning duo,
coming soon.

THE DOCTOR'S UNEXPECTED FAMILY

BY
LILIAN DARCY

First published in Great Britain 2004
Large Print edition 2004
Harlequin Mills & Boon Limited,
Eton House, 18-24 Paradise Road,
Richmond, Surrey TW9 1SR

© Lilian Darcy 2004

ISBN 0 263 18171 5

Set in Times Roman 16½ on 17½ pt.
17-1104-49158

Printed and bound in Great Britain
by Antony Rowe Ltd, Chippenham, Wiltshire

CHAPTER ONE

'I CANNOT emphasise strongly enough how important it is that we hang onto this man.'

Dr Robinson—dear Tom—never seemed able to emphasise anything strongly enough, Caroline mused, although he certainly tried. Having gathered the staff of his small department for an informal Friday afternoon meeting in his office, he now sat on the corner of his desk, with his thick, greying brows knitted and a fist pounding into his palm at rhythmic intervals as he spoke, in quest of that ever-elusive emphasis.

As usual, Caroline's fingers itched for a pair of tweezers with which to permanently unknit the brows, and she thought guiltily, My mind is wandering.

It wandered a little more as Dr Robinson spoke of signing Declan McCulloch up for tennis, inviting him over for meals and befriending his girlfriend on the weekends when she came down from Sydney to stay.

'And, of course, Caroline—' Dr Robinson's emphasis suddenly switched to her and she twitched and sat up straighter '—you'll have a particular role to play in this.'

She blinked. 'Oh, I will?'

'Isn't he renting your parents' house?'

'Um, yes.'

'Presumably they've left it in immaculate condition.'

'Well, yes, Tom…'

'But if are any problems—appliances breaking down, and so forth…'

'Yes, of course. I'll be the one to call a repair man.'

'Promptly.'

'Promptly,' she agreed. She was very fond of Tom Robinson, but he had an increasing tendency to paw at a subject like a dog pawing at a bone.

'And I think it would be an excellent gesture if you'd bring a casserole to welcome him, and perhaps stock the pantry with some basic supplies.'

'Right,' she murmured. 'I suppose I could.'

Natalia shifted and fiddled with her rings. Steph yawned, and surreptitiously checked a note scribbled in her diary. Mary took a look out of the window at the weather.

Tom frowned again, and looked sincerely anxious. 'Please, take this seriously, everyone,' he said.

Caroline took a deep breath and stepped into the breach.

'I think we are, Tom,' she said, 'and I take your point about making him and his girlfriend welcome. Glenfallon is a welcoming sort of place by nature, I always think. But we have to be realistic, don't we? He's here because, as a non-Australian doctor, the only way he can practise before he sits his Australian exams is by working in a designated Area of Need, which means the country, not the city.'

'If we can settle him thoroughly enough here. He's thirty-six. Ready, you'd think. To put down roots, start a family...'

'He's not the only one we have to consider, that's the problem. His girlfriend works in television, my mother says. There won't be any employment prospects for her here, which means that, no matter how much he warms to the place, he's highly unlikely to stay beyond the year, or at most the two years, he'll spend preparing for the exams.'

'Let's take a more positive attitude than that, Caroline,' Tom answered with spirit. He slid off the desk and stood up, and Caroline realised for the first time that his tall, gangly body had begun to stoop. He was growing old. 'Perhaps their relationship won't last!'

Everyone laughed, as if Dr Robinson had been joking, but Caroline thought, No, he means it. I know him too well! He's not going to let it go, he's going to fret over it, and his perspective is too narrow. I hope I'm not going to regret that Mum and Dad rented Dr McCulloch the house. Could I get Chris to do the liaising?

She suppressed a sigh. No, that wouldn't be fair. Her brother had married a sheep farmer's daughter, and was settled on the huge property that Sandie had inherited from her parents, which lay a hundred and twenty kilometres to the north-west. Chris or Sandie came into town fairly often, but Caroline didn't want to add to the long list of errands they always had when they were here.

Tom had a couple more items to cover on his informal agenda, then his staff scattered to tidy their desks for the weekend. Tom presided over a group of six women at the moment—a secretary, three lab technicians and two cyto technicians. Caroline was one of the latter, along with Natalia, who worked only part time. Declan McCulloch's arrival, as a much-needed second pathologist, would shift the gender balance just a little in Tom's favour.

Caroline's phone rang just as she was about to switch off her microscope. Probably Josh, she thought as she picked it up. At the beginning of the school year, six weeks ago, he'd announced that he wasn't going to after-school care any more. He wanted his own house key, and he'd ride his bike home and look after himself, on the days he wasn't invited to a friend's.

She had been a little nervous and a little sceptical, but had agreed to give the plan a trial run. She had a reliable neighbour to keep an eye on him, and so far she was pleased and proud at the way he handled his new independence. Josh was eleven, a little vague and disorganised at times, but basically sensible.

A couple of times a week, however, she'd get a phone call from him at around this hour. 'Can I have an ice cream from the freezer? It's really hot!' was the usual reason for the call, and it was hot again today, so…

She had a smile in her voice as she put the receiver to her ear and said a warm and casual, 'Hi.'

The resonant silence at the far end of the line told her this wasn't Josh even before an unfamiliar male voice asked cautiously, 'Am I speaking to Caroline Archer?'

'Oh. Yes. You are. I'm sorry.'

The voice might be unfamiliar, but she had little doubt as to who it was. That Irish accent was as curly and intricate to her ears as lines of a handwritten musical score. It had to be—

'Declan McCulloch, phoning from Sydney. Your parents gave me this number.'

'Of course they did.' Mum and Dad had already left for the Gold Coast, and she would be acting on their behalf in matters concerning their house from now on. 'I'm sorry, I thought it would be my son. Please, tell me how I can help you, Dr McCulloch,' she finished, with a passable degree of courtesy and calm.

'I'm hoping to arrange a time tomorrow when my partner can look over the house with you. Would that be possible?'

'Yes, it would be fine.' The Irish accent threw her more than it should have.

'Unfortunately, I can't be there myself, but Suzy was hoping to meet you at the house at around nine-thirty or ten, if that suits.'

'Yes, OK, nine-thirty…' Caroline frantically tried to remember what time Josh's soccer game started. Eleven? 'Nine-thirty would be fine.'

If the game was at ten, she'd have to—

'And I should be arriving in the late afternoon with our things.'

'So you're actually moving in tomorrow?'

Go shopping. Make casserole. Stock pantry. She'd have to do all this tonight. Tom was right. Make both of them as welcome as possible, so that when the new pathologist did leave after a year or two it wouldn't be anyone's fault, and especially not hers.

'Hoping to, if that's all right,' Declan McCulloch said. 'Technically, our lease started today, I believe.'

The tone had a tiny bit of a tease in it, as if he was the kind of man who used humour and warmth to get what he wanted, never anger or the leverage of power. The lease started today, so he could move in whenever he wanted, could he not? And couldn't he get her to agree to this fact without a fuss?

Or was this a little too much to conclude about his way of operating from one brief statement?

'Of course,' Caroline answered him.

She almost said something about the casserole, but managed to refrain. He rang off, leaving her to realise for the first time that his tenancy of her parents' house might put her in a very awkward position when they had to work together as well. He'd dialled her direct line and she'd replied with that casual, 'Hi.' As a result, Dr McCulloch probably didn't realise that one of the cyto technicians who'd be reporting to him in his new position at Glenfallon hospital was also, in effect, his landlady.

Looking up, she found Tom Robinson leaning in the doorway. 'Was that—?'

'Dr McCulloch, yes.'

'How did he sound? Was there a problem? Did you manage to—?'

'Tom, you have to relax about this!' she cut in gently.

He sighed. 'I can't. Listen, can I talk to you for a minute?'

'Of course.'

He came into her office and shut the door. 'The thing is—and I haven't told anyone this yet so, please, keep it to yourself—I want to take early retirement within the next year or two.' He was fifty-eight, Caroline knew. 'Eileen's mother in Melbourne is getting very frail, and with three of the four grandchildren down there, too, Eileen is very torn. She's been spending more and more time there, and I miss her—to a stupid extent, really—when she's gone.' His voice went foggy. 'We can't go on splitting our energies between Glenfallon and Melbourne.'

'Oh, Tom!'

'But I won't go—' he spoke more firmly now '—until there's a second pathologist who is good and competent and committed, and already in place. This Declan McCulloch could be the man, and if there's the slightest chance we can keep him after he's passed his Australian exams, then we have to—'

'I understand. I'll do my best, Tom, I really will.'

She arrived home twenty minutes later, to find a line of tiny brown ants feasting on the sweet residue left by the ice-cream stick Josh had abandoned on the kitchen benchtop.

'I decided there was no point in bothering you at work about having an ice cream when you always say yes,' he told her, and they had a little discussion about the problem of the ants when the benchtop wasn't left clean.

She flung some frozen fish pieces and shoe-string potato fries in the oven, made a salad and composed a shopping list, and Josh accompanied her to the supermarket without protest after they'd eaten. He was a good kid, and old enough now to be much more of a companion and a help to her than he had been when little.

Caroline had been divorced from Josh's father for almost ten years. Robert had a distant involvement with his son, and high expectations of him. To what extent Josh would be required to follow in his father's footsteps was an issue that loomed nearer. He would be starting high school next year.

The two of them delivered the 'basic supplies' for Dr McCulloch and his girlfriend to their rented pantry and fridge, and while Josh was in bed with a book Caroline made the casserole and had it slowly simmering in the oven by the time Josh turned his reading lamp off at nine o'clock.

Unfortunately, despite this impressive degree of efficiency and organisation, she forgot to check the time of his soccer game until the next morning. The game began at ten, not eleven.

'I'm so sorry I'm late.' Caroline held out the covered casserole dish to Dr McCulloch's girlfriend as a peace offering.

She felt as if Tom were an invisible presence just behind her, listening to everything she said and assessing it for the appropriate degree of *welcomingness*, so to speak. She was also far too conscious of the house's dated 1940s red-brick front. The girlfriend had been grimacing at the house, a minute ago, as she'd prowled around the front garden.

Mum and Dad's place was a bit of a secret treasure, as it looked bland and boring from the front but was lovely once you got inside. She hoped Dr McCulloch's girlfriend hadn't already made up her mind to dislike it.

'Is this for us?' The girlfriend took the casserole dish. The way Caroline held it out, she had little choice. 'You didn't have to.'

She didn't look through the glass lid, or display any other sign of appreciation, and

Caroline had the uncomfortable feeling that perhaps chicken and mushroom casseroles were very old-fashioned and countrified, and that this one might be discarded tonight in favour of take-away Thai from Glenfallon's recently opened House of Siam restaurant.

The girlfriend—Suzy—looked very city-ish to Caroline's eye, which was an idiotic way to look at her, as plenty of women in Glenfallon had short, spiky blonde hair, even if most of them didn't wear expensive designer casuals on a Saturday morning.

OK, so Suzy Screenwriter wasn't city-ish, she was just fashion-conscious and skinny and probably the right side of thirty.

While I'm not.

Any of those things.

Caroline unlocked the front door and they went inside. The house felt a little stuffy, which it wouldn't have done if she'd been able to get here before Suzy to open up. 'My son's soccer game was earlier than I thought,' she explained, throwing open windows in the lounge-room and bathroom.

'Hmm,' Suzy Screenwriter said, not interested.

I mustn't call her Suzy Screenwriter, Caroline realised, even in my head, because it'll make me start disliking her, and that wouldn't be helpful. I have to love her to death. We have to be best friends. She has to be crazy about the whole town.

'You can put the casserole in the fridge,' she offered. 'I stocked it last night with a few basics, in case you don't get a chance to shop for a couple of days.'

'I suppose the shops are all closed on the weekends anyway, aren't they?'

'Oh, no, we're quite well catered for in that area. There's a huge supermarket near...'

Suzy Screenwriter wasn't listening. She'd reached the kitchen, which Mum and Dad had had remodelled only last year, opening it up to a new sun-room that jutted into the green frenzy of the back garden. 'There's a dishwasher, I hope?'

Suzy looked around the kitchen, spotted it and looked relieved. Then she smiled, as if realising that she should come across a little more warmly. 'Could I see the other rooms, please, before we get onto the detail of how everything works?'

'Of course.'

'When I move down here, you see, I'm going to start work on a major novel. Dec has told me there's a room with a view of the garden for my office. I hope it feels right. I'm so looking forward to the chance of getting some real writing done. The solitude and lack of distractions in a place like this will be a great discipline for me.'

'I can imagine, yes. Let me show you the room, then. Will you be moving down soon?'

'Not as soon as I'd like. Unfortunately I have a TV drama series I'm committed to in Sydney until later in the year. Dec will come up as often as he can, and I'll come down here for extended weekends. We're not looking forward to that, but there's no choice with these arcane regulations about where foreign doctors can practise.'

She wandered through the rooms as she spoke, and concluded after a few minutes, 'Dec's right. This is perfect.' Circling back to the room she planned to use as an office, she narrowed her eyes, as if imagining desk and computer and bookshelves in place, then gave another satisfied nod.

She had a casual air of confidence that Caroline envied, if she was honest—confidence in her own ability to write 'a major novel', in her plan to make the six-hour drive from Sydney for frequent weekends, in her relationship with 'Dec'.

Did I ever have that? Caroline wondered to herself. Even before things went pear-shaped with Robert, and with my medical career? I'm not sure that I did.

'Right, I'll have the lessons on the dishwasher and the washing-machine now, thanks, Caroline,' Suzy said, and Caroline was able to hand over the keys in time to catch the second half of Josh's game.

'How did it go with the casserole?' Tom asked at eight o'clock on Monday morning. 'Did the girlfriend like the house? And the town? And did you stock the pantry?'

'I stocked the pantry and the fridge, although my idea of the basics might be completely different from theirs,' Caroline told her boss.

'Surely not,' he answered. He'd summoned her into his office the moment she'd arrived, with an impatient and conspiratorial air that made her want to giggle. Evidently, the new pathologist was expected to darken their doorway at any moment, so there was no time to lose. 'Basics are basics, aren't they?'

'Well, you know, they might want pâté instead of margarine, Turkish pide bread instead of sliced white. They could be on some kind of diet.'

Tom looked horrified. 'I hadn't thought of that.'

'But even if they are, they'd have to appreciate the thought.'

'True. And did he appreciate the casserole?'

'I don't know. I haven't laid eyes on him. I gave it to her. Suzy Screenwriter.' Damn. 'Suzy...Vaughan, it is. I got the feeling she might have thought it was, well, too home-made.'

'But that's what we're about, Caroline. A country welcome, a home-made atmosphere. I know you think I'm going overboard on this.'

'I don't, really. I understand, Tom. I'm going overboard, too. I'd have appreciated a home-made casserole, if it was me. Probably they did, too.'

'I'm not so concerned about her, to be honest.' He lowered his voice. 'Really, you're right about her not finding employment here.

We're going to, seriously, have to hope that she drops out of the picture.'

'Oh, no, that's the one piece of good news. She's going to write a novel, so that makes her much more portable.'

'It does, doesn't it?' His face brightened. 'Perfect!'

'She's excited about the prospect of solitude in Glenfallon, and the lack of distractions.'

'Translation—the boredom?' A twinkle appeared in Dr Robinson's eye, beneath the big brows.

'I'm pinning big hopes on that novel,' Caroline answered, and her statement was punctuated by a knock at the door.

'That's him,' Dr Robinson mouthed.

Having had her curiosity and her expectations built up by several weeks of rumours concerning the new pathologist, not to mention a curly Irish accent on the phone and three days of worrying about the casserole, the kitchen supplies and the screenwriting girlfriend, Caroline found she was holding her breath and squeezing her hands into damp fists.

They all wanted this new appointment to be a success. With the spectre of health-funding cuts and consolidation of services, Glenfallon

Hospital needed to grow if it was to serve its community adequately. Declan McCulloch was just a single link in the chain, but to this department he was a crucial one.

Tom cleared his throat. 'Come in,' he called, and the door opened.

A tall, strong, easy-moving male figure appeared, with a face already smiling, and an air about him of already knowing how much he was wanted here. For some reason, Caroline's heart at once began to beat faster.

CHAPTER TWO

IF ANYONE had told Declan McCulloch, this time last year, that he'd be walking into a small pathology department in rural Australia on a morning in mid-March for his first day on the job, he'd have laughed at them.

Moving to Australia? When he'd finished his specialist training and was set up in London, making his parents proud? When he'd tucked himself beneath the wing of a success-ful professional mentor and was on track for a stellar career? No, thanks!

But he hadn't reckoned on Suzy, or on his own willingness to be, effectively, swept off his feet. The whole thing still surprised him, when he thought back on it.

They'd met in a London pub. Across a crowded room kind of thing. 'I'm a sucker for an Irish accent,' she'd told him, in a very at-tractive accent of her own. She'd made all the moves. He hadn't been used to that, and he'd liked it, loved her brash confidence. After so much hard work to get where he was in his profession, Suzy had brightened his world like an exotic cocktail on a tropical beach. He must have been restless without even realising it.

They'd slept together immediately.

Seriously! That night.

Her idea. Her moves.

He had been innocent enough, old-fashioned enough, that her willingness to take it so far, so soon, had shocked him. He would have been content to wait. He'd even wondered since that night whether he should have gone with a more cautious instinct to put on the brakes for a week or two. But how could he have politely declined such a dazzling invitation, when it had seemed to answer such a hunger in him?

There was a wicked, competitive aura to their relationship, a sense that both of them were playing a delicious and sometimes dangerous game. Chess, or fencing. She'd mentioned Sydney only a few weeks after they'd met. 'You'd love it.' He hadn't taken her seriously at that point. Not at all. Why on earth would a medical specialist want to leave London?

And then she'd been offered the scriptwriting job for the drama series. Her agent in

Sydney had told her she would be crazy to turn it down. She'd been trying to make a career as a playwright and screenwriter in London, but after some months nothing much had happened, while the work in Sydney had been a good, concrete offer that could lead to bigger things. She had taken her agent's advice and accepted.

More seriously and more urgently, she'd told him again, 'You'd really love Sydney,' and she'd painted her word pictures in such beautiful colours that he'd quickly gone from laughing at her—Sydney was out of the question!—to talking with her about how it could be managed. He had no personal ties to London. He hadn't bought real estate. None of his siblings lived here. The closest was his sister Maeve, in Scotland.

'And if it doesn't work out, you can always come back,' Suzy had said.

True. He'd taken a two-year leave of absence from his position at the hospital. His boats were not burned.

Oddly, the decision hadn't been set in stone until they'd discovered that he couldn't actually live in Sydney at all, or at least not for the first year or two, if he wanted to work at the same time. He'd always reacted badly to being told that something was impossible. The red tape surrounding the possibility of following Suzy to Australia had become a reason to carry through with the idea, not a reason to let it go.

Suzy had flown home to start work on her TV series three months before he'd been able to wind up his life in London and join her. He'd then spent two summer months lazing on Bondi beach and playing housekeeper to her breadwinner while they'd got to know each other in a different environment, and now he was here.

Ready for it, actually.

He wasn't from a moneyed background as Suzy was. He'd worked hard for everything he had, and he'd never taken a two-month break before. To be honest, after the first couple of weeks he'd had to consciously fill his days in order not to be bored. He'd learned to surf, learned to cook and had started to prepare for the onerous Australian exams which even a fully qualified London specialist couldn't take lightly.

And now he was here.

'Declan!' Tom Robinson said. He took three strides across his grey-walled and rather spartan office and held out his hand, pumped Declan's heartily. 'Good to see you! Settled in? Happy with everything? Finding your way around town? Do tell Caroline if you have any problems with the house, won't you?'

Tom indicated the woman who stood in the background. In strictest truth, this office wasn't large enough to contain a background, but if there had been one, Declan had no doubt that Caroline would have been standing as deep in it as she could get.

'Caroline Archer, Declan McCulloch,' Tom added.

Wearing a patterned navy blouse and plain navy skirt as a uniform, she had her arms folded across her chest in a gesture that said, Please don't shake my hand. Her backside was pressed against the edge of Tom's desk. Had the desk not been there, she would have backed herself as far as the wall.

'In practical terms, she's your landlady,' Tom explained.

I suppose I did look a little confused at the sight of her, Declan thought.

He was more confused now. Dr Robinson had invited his new landlady in to the department to greet him on his first day at work? Why?

'My parents own the house,' Caroline explained.

She was pretty when her cheeks were flushed. She had dark, straight, shiny hair folded up into a big clip at the back, green eyes and a figure that most women would consider too plump. Most men wouldn't, since it was plump in all the best places.

'Right,' Declan answered helpfully.

'She's also one of our cyto technicians, and a very good one, as you'll soon discover.'

'OK, now it's all falling into place.'

'Good,' Caroline said. 'I realised, of course, that I should have explained on the phone the other day.'

'Well, I did recognise that it was a hospital number I'd dialled, but I had no idea it was going to be in my own department,' Declan said.

'Right, OK.' She smiled. Tom smiled. Declan decided to smile, too, to blend in with the local crowd.

'No problems with the house?' Caroline said.

'No, everything was fine. The chicken thing

was delicious. You didn't have to do that for us.'

'We're anxious to have you settle in comfortably, Declan,' Tom said.

Too anxious, and not hiding it successfully. *Caroline thinks so as well.*

Their eyes locked together for a moment, and in hers he saw a pained expression that he understood. Relax, he tried to tell her with his eyes and his smile. Tom means well, and I can see that, and I'm not going to put you in an awkward position here at work, or with the house.

Not that a glance and a quirk of the lips could achieve as much communication as that. Something must have got through, however, because she did relax and she looked grateful. She had a lovely smile—not dazzling but misty soft, quiet. It was a smile you could trust.

'Well,' Tom said, 'let me take you round, show you the place, introduce you. Caroline, could you get out the slides for the case I mentioned earlier? The one I wanted to show him?'

'Yes, the slide tray's already on my desk.'

Caroline let the two men leave first, and

took a moment to wipe her damp hands on her skirt after they'd done so.

'What on earth must he think of us?' she muttered.

Well, she could answer that question.

He thinks we're quaint and funny and well-meaning, and that he's going to have to be very tactful and gentle with us, and of course he's right. Meanwhile, what do we think of him? I wonder.

He was certainly good-looking. He wasn't as tall as Tom but he was better proportioned, with broad, strong shoulders and solid packs of muscle softening the contours of an otherwise lean frame.

His eyes were a soft grey-blue, and his hair was the kind of brown that could secretly begin to turn grey without anyone noticing for a good while. Caroline was an authority on this issue, because hers wasn't that kind of brown at all. It was too dark, the grey hairs showed, and she'd had to pick out a few of them lately.

She was thirty-four, not anywhere near old enough for grey hairs. Dr McCulloch must be around the same age. If she hadn't known he was Irish, she'd have guessed him to be younger, on the strength of his skin. An Australian man in his mid-thirties would have had crow's feet, but Dr McCulloch didn't. He had good skin—smooth, even toned, the slightest of tans and the subtlest of freckles, legacy of his first Australian summer, she guessed.

On first assessment, too, he had an Irish charm that went beyond his good looks and might have seemed like a cliché. All Irishmen were supposed to be charming, weren't they? Charming and silver-tongued. Except that the charm in this one was tempered by a degree of caution and inner quiet which made him seem a little bit different.

Way too much to conclude after all of three minutes' acquaintance. But first impressions did count. On the strength of this one, Dr Declan McCulloch would be all right. If he stayed.

Leaving Tom Robinson's office, Caroline heard her boss's voice coming from along the corridor. He'd dropped back into his hearty, making-you-feel-welcome tone. She heard her fellow cyto tech, Natalia Akhmanov, give a laugh on cue. Like everyone else, she was doing exactly as ordered and trying far too hard.

I'm going to start work, Caroline decided. I'm going to forget the man is even here.

She made herself a cup of coffee, greeted Natalia as she came towards their shared office and sat down at her desk. She switched on her microscope and computer, and the hard drive began to hum.

'This lot will keep us busy all morning,' Natalia said.

'And me all afternoon as well,' Caroline agreed.

Their in-box was already piled with slide trays. A high percentage of their work consisted of Pap smears, but there could also be urine, sputum and cerebrospinal fluid samples, all of them prepared and logged into the computer by lab technicians Mary, Julianne and Irena.

They began their work in an atmosphere of focused silence. Down the corridor came the faint sound of laughter from the lab technicians, punctuating the tap of Natalia's computer keys. A glass slide clicked and squeaked as Caroline slid it beneath her microscope.

With an efficiency that came from years of practice, she rolled the control knob between finger and thumb, bringing different areas of the sample into view. Stained with red and blue pigments that ended up as a range of pink, purple and blue tones, the cells were oddly beautiful in the round window of light. If you didn't know what they were, you might think they were fabric patterns or abstract paintings.

It was her job to know what they were, however—to recognise tell-tale signs of abnormality in the structure or shape or staining of a cell. This was what she loved about her job—its sense of familiarity, its regular boundaries and just the odd occasion when it wasn't familiar and the boundaries weren't regular, so that she didn't ever get too complacent.

She spent ten minutes on the first slide, marking clusters of normal cervix cells with a tiny blue dot of acrylic artist's ink. She would use white dots to mark any abnormal cells, but white wasn't necessary on this test because everything looked fine. Their rate of abnormal Pap smears was, very roughly, one in ten.

'Can you put the Mitchell case into the multi-header for me, Caroline?' Dr Robinson said behind her, fifteen minutes later.

'Of course.' She went to the larger microscope in the middle of the room, switched it on and slid in one of the series of slides showing seventy-two-year-old Roy Mitchell's cere-brospinal fluid. The multi-header microscope had four eyepieces, and was used to review abnormal samples as a group.

'I love the view from our windows, here, Declan,' her boss said behind her, as she looked into the eyepiece and searched for the most interesting area on the slide. 'The morning light through the eucalyptus trees, and the sunsets we sometimes get.'

For heaven's sake, Tom, stop selling the place to him! she wanted to say. Stop trying so hard!

Instead, she tried too hard, herself, to get the slide positioned quickly, as a way of getting Tom to stop rhapsodising about sunsets. Damn! She'd flicked the slide tray's control too far around and lost the section she was looking for.

Filling in time, Tom said to the new pathologist, 'It's an unusual case, Declan, and I thought you might like to have a look at it. You'll find, you see, that even though we're a small department we do get a wide range of interesting things to look at. Some very nice stuff. There's more patient contact than you'd get in a large hospital or private lab, too, and—

Anyway,' he interrupted himself, 'let's take a look at this lovely sample. Caroline?'

'Almost got it, I think.' Disciplining herself to forget that Declan McCulloch's hip, clad in dark linen blend, stood just beyond her peripheral vision, she concentrated and positioned the slide at last. 'There!' She pushed her chair back in relief and stood up, guessing that Tom would want the central control position now.

Her boss had crowded so close behind her, however, that she had to sidle past Declan McCulloch before he and Tom could sit down. Declan's legs brushed her skirt. He apologised, and so did she.

Seated, he peered into one of the multi-header's auxiliary eyepieces, waiting for Tom, and she watched his neck stretch as he leaned forward. His hair finished above his collar in little waves that looked soft against his skin, and the knobs of his vertebrae were straight and even.

Apparently, Tom wasn't happy with the particular cell cluster she'd chosen, and twiddled the positioning knob for some seconds before he found what he wanted. Declan sat opposite her, peering into another eyepiece, while Natalia took up the last available position.

They all enjoyed the opportunity to look at interesting slides as a group.

'Ah, yes, now, this one's better,' Tom said. He rolled another knob between his fingers, bringing up a tiny, bright golden arrow to indicate the group of cells he was looking at. 'Declan?'

'Yes, you're right,' he said, after a moment. 'Lovely.'

His tone made Caroline think of the Queen on a royal tour, politely admiring a floral arrangement created in her honour. How quaint, he was probably thinking, that these colonial medical people should try so hard to provide him with interesting examples of malignant cells on his very first day.

'Except, of course, that this patient is not going to live beyond the end of the year,' she said in a mild tone. She stood up from the multi-header and went back to her own microscope. She brought up her current case on the computer and began to key in the required information without troubling to see how the two doctors had taken her statement.

She'd aimed it at Tom. He really couldn't talk about a slide like this being 'a lovely sample' in the hope of impressing the new man.

But her comment had actually sounded more like a criticism of Dr McCulloch's use of 'lovely', although she'd recognised the gentle mockery in the Irish pathologist's voice and knew he'd echoed his new boss deliberately.

'You're right, Caroline,' Dr McCulloch said behind her, and she turned from the screen to face him, swivelling on her wheeled chair. 'They're not just cells. There's a doctor out there with some bad news to break when he gets the report on this one, Tom.'

'Not necessarily a local doctor either,' Tom answered, oblivious to the mild reproach. 'We have a large catchment area here. Some days you'll speak on the phone to a GP who might be a hundred miles away, or more, which is probably not an experience you've had in London.'

Still speaking with enthusiasm about his department, Tom walked Declan McCulloch along to his new office. Caroline turned gratefully back to her work.

After four hours and a couple of trips along to the lab or across to Tom's office with questions, a spot high on her spine had begun to ache and she was ready to tackle some stretching exercises before lunch. New ergonomic chairs were on order, but they hadn't arrived yet. Natalia often had problems with her back, too. It was tiring to spend so many hours over a microscope, and they couldn't afford to let aches and pains compromise the accuracy of their screening. The task took full concentration.

She leaned back, arched her spine, pushed her wheeled chair away from the desk and stretched her arms behind her. At that moment, Tom and Dr McCulloch came past the cyto techs' office, stopping in the doorway. Her unselfconscious and cat-like stretch was suddenly on public display.

'I'm taking Declan to lunch in town,' Tom said. 'I think he'll be pleasantly surprised at the standard of the Glenfallon Bakery, particularly if we go through into the Old Bank section.'

'Lovely!' Caroline answered, then almost bit her tongue.

Just how lovely could everything in this town get?

'Would you like to come?' the Irishman suggested. His smile twinkled in her direction.

Flustered, she answered, 'Thanks, but I'm already booked for the hospital café with Natalia.'

Dr McCulloch shrugged, clicked his tongue and quirked the corner of his mouth downward. 'That's too bad.'

Caroline realised too late that his suggestion hadn't been just a piece of politeness. He'd actively wanted a third party to water down the intensity of Tom's overpowering enthusiasm.

Oh, Tom, you dear, desperate man! We'll be lucky to keep the poor bloke for six months at this rate, she thought as her boss shepherded the new recruit out of the department and down the stairs.

CHAPTER THREE

'I SHOULD have said no to Tom,' Caroline muttered to herself, as she pulled up in front of her parents' house at just after five. 'I should have used Josh as an excuse. I really don't want to be doing this!'

'Declan left early,' Tom had told her half an hour before. 'He had more unpacking to do. Just drop in on your way home, very casually, could you? To make sure everything's all right? You can mention the barbecue idea, too. Natalia's happy to have it at her place, she says.'

'You couldn't mention it to him yourself tomorrow?'

'The sooner the better,' Tom had replied decisively, 'in case he makes other plans.'

'Or by phone?'

'Much better in person. Flexible, though, Caroline. If he wants Suzy included, and if she's not coming down this weekend, suggest the next.'

'All right,' she'd answered, feeling Tom's urgency and understanding it, even though she knew he was going about this all wrong.

She really didn't have an excuse not to call in on Dr McCulloch, unfortunately. Josh had gym after school on Mondays, and a joint science project to work on with the same friend, Rohan, who also went to gym. Rohan's mother had suggested that she pick both boys up and that Josh stay for dinner after he and Rohan had worked on the project.

Not that Declan McCulloch knew about this plan, so she could fib if she needed to—if lurching through her script about the house and the barbecue invitation just got too horribly awkward—and could use Josh as an excuse. It was one of the rare benefits of being a single parent.

And with luck the man wouldn't even be home…

He was.

'Hi,' she bleated, when he appeared at the door in answer to her knock.

'Hi, yourself.' Although he flashed a crooked smile, he didn't look particularly overjoyed to see her.

Naturally enough.

He'd changed out of his professional trousers and shirt and wore a pair of ragged, snug-fitting jeans, athletic shoes and a black T-shirt, obviously with the intention of hefting boxes around. Caroline didn't know if Suzy was still in town, hefting boxes too. Either way, her own presence was an intrusion.

'Come in,' he added, after a moment.

He wore his hair longish on top and it rippled in lazy, untidy waves over his nicely shaped head, mussed up by the work he'd been doing. He had a dust mark on his cheek, and he must have felt it because he pulled a white tissue from his back pocket and brushed at it, frowning, as he waited for her to speak.

'Look, I won't,' she answered. 'I just dropped in to make sure everything was working properly, and that you and Suzy are happy. With the house,' she added, as if he might otherwise have thought she was asking about the state of their relationship.

'Everything's fine,' he said. 'Suzy went back this morning. She has script meetings the rest of the week. But, no, we're fine, there's hot water coming out of the taps and cold air in the fridge, and what more could we need?'

'Good. That's great.'

'Oh, but one thing. Is there somewhere I can store our boxes once they're empty?' His accent stretched the last word out, and made it flutter on his tongue. Caroline could have closed her eyes and listened to him speaking the way she listened to music. 'Up in the ceiling? Or is the garage dry enough when it rains? I'll flatten them, and they won't take up a lot of room, but I want to hang onto them.'

For the next two years.

Until he and Suzy moved back to Sydney.

Tom was chasing the pot of gold at the end of the rainbow on this one.

'That's fine,' she answered vaguely, washed with a flood of disappointment, for Tom's sake. 'I think the garage stays dry and, yes, there's a big hatch in the laundry ceiling. Wherever you like.'

'Great.'

'There's a long aluminium ladder in the garage. You could lay that flat on the concrete and sit the boxes on top. That would let some air circulate underneath, keep the damp and the beetles from getting to them.'

'I'll do that, that's a good idea. Thanks.'

Caroline could see that, as far as he was concerned, the conversation had reached the end-game.

'Um,' she said. 'I'm supposed to invite you to a barbecue.'

'Supposed to?'

'Tom. Well, we discussed it. All of us. At Natalia's. A welcome from the department, a chance to meet some other people from the hospital, as well as our families. This weekend, or next, depending on whether Suzy's down, because, of course, we want to welcome her as well, make her part of the—'

Stop, Caroline.

'I'm not sure when she'll be down, unfortunately,' he said. A small furrow had appeared in his forehead between a pair of well-separated brows. It gave him a forbidding look, and suggested the strength of will that lay beneath the polite, accommodating manner. 'It depends on her rewrites, whether they're major or minor, and when they're due, and whether she has to have another meeting about them. Writer stuff. Can I let you know?'

'Let Tom know.'

'Could you let Tom know, as well, Caroline, that he can relax a little bit?' His expression stretched into an appeal, almost causing a dimple in one cheek. 'I'm feeling somewhat—'

More than somewhat, she could tell.

'Oh, swamped, smothered, I know!' She pressed her hands to her face, cheeks burning. 'Please, let me apologise on his behalf. He means well, but sometimes he can't let things go. Please, take it with a grain of salt, and don't let it put you off, because we're all so much hoping that you'll settle— Oh, crumbs! Bloody hell! I'm doing it too now, aren't I? As bad as he is!'

She looked up at him, gave a desperate, upside-down grin and spread her arms in a helpless gesture.

'Hey, now,' he said gently, his voice like sweet milk, fresh from the cow. 'This is ridiculous. Why don't you come in? Seriously, and have a glass of wine. Or a beer, if you're that way inclined. I have both.'

'No, I—' Can easily pretend that I have to pick up Josh.

'I mean it. Sorry I didn't insist on it at first. I shouldn't tar you with Tom's brush. You won't spend the next hour impersonating a Glenfallon travel brochure, will you?'

'Oh, no! Did Tom—?'

'Quite a long travel brochure, too. Three-quarters of an hour, over lunch. Wineries, olive groves, Carrawirra National Park...'

'Oh, no, how dreadful!'

She laughed, because he was laughing, too. His eyes looked more blue than grey when he laughed, and they twinkled. Thank goodness he had a sense of humour!

'Come on,' he said, and she followed him into the house, while he did a terrible, hysterical imitation of Tom's educated Australian voice extolling the delights of Glenfallon in fluent brochure-ese. 'Nestled in the rolling hills that slope towards the fertile green of award-winning vineyards lies— White, red or amber?' he interrupted himself.

'Oh, white. Would be lovely.'

'Already chilled.' He opened the fridge and flourished a bottle. 'Verdelho. Suzy and I did a winery tour yesterday, so it's local.'

'The Leader Buslines tour, was it? Some friends and I did that last year.'

'I thought it was only for tourists.'

'It is, but we did it anyway. It shouldn't be just for tourists. It was a lot of fun, and we learned enough about wine for me to pretend I know what a Verdelho is.'

'You know about as much as me, then. Sun-room?'

She'd noticed coming through from the front door that he and Suzy had the rather small, dark lounge-room set up as his study, since Suzy had nabbed the room with the garden view for hers. Now, coming into the sun-room, she found that this was where they intended the focus of the house to be, and it worked well this way.

They had their music system set up as well as a television. Couches, armchairs and end-tables were casually arranged to face the French windows that opened onto a paved patio. On the patio, they'd placed a gas bar-becue and some freshly potted orange trees with the nursery tags still attached. They must have bought them on the weekend.

Declan's time in Glenfallon might only be temporary, but he still considered it worth-while to create a feeling of home here. Caroline liked that. It gave her a tiny bit of hope on Tom's behalf.

As if he'd read her mind, Declan asked, 'Tell me about Tom. Tell me why he's per-secuting me like this.' He grinned to soften his statement, and she grinned back, finding his face very easy to watch.

As she mentally scrambled to put her answer together, he sank into the striped and padded cushions of a cane couch, and leaned forward to the coffee-table where he'd placed the wine. Watching knotted arm muscles stretch out, and lean fingers twist the corkscrew, she told him simply, 'He'd like you to put down roots and stay forever.'

'He must know that's unlikely.' The cork came out of the bottle neck with a resonant *thlop*, and straw-coloured wine gurgled into the two stemmed glasses. Like a wine waiter, Declan gave a deft twist to the bottle so that it didn't drip, and set it on the long, low coffee-table beside a wooden bowl filled with what he probably called 'crisps'.

'Rationally, yes,' Caroline answered. 'But we need two pathologists now. Tom himself...' She hesitated, weighing Tom's request for confidentiality against the need to explain his over-the-top behaviour. 'Will obviously have to retire eventually, and he cares too much about the department to be able to contemplate leaving it in the hands of someone who's not right. Or, worse, leaving before there's a replacement in view at all.'

'Given the chronic shortage of medical specialists in rural Australia, right?' He stood up and stretched across the coffee-table to give her the wine. She took care that their fingers didn't touch.

'Yes.'

'It seems like a nice town,' he offered.

'It is. It's lovely. But I can see that your personal circumstances don't fit what Tom wants. I'll try to make sure he doesn't persecute you any further.'

'Don't worry about it. As long as I've got someone to share a laugh with when he starts on the Tidy Town of the Year routine.'

'Me? Laugh with me?'

'If you don't mind.' He sat down, and their eyes met once more and held for a moment.

'I never mind a good laugh,' she told him. 'But I'm fond of Tom. Don't be unkind.'

'I'm sorry that you think I would.'

'I don't think that. Not necessarily. But I don't know you very well yet, so...'

After an hour, she knew him better, although she couldn't have described very clearly what she'd learned. That he listened well. That he took his work seriously. That he liked its measured pace, and the opportunities it offered for solitude.

'You don't like actual, breathing patients?'

'Oh, I do. Patients—people—are fascinating. But I can overdose on them if I'm not careful. The other specialty I considered was emergency medicine, but it was too...potent, or something. I thrived on my emergency stints during training, but in the long term it would have burned me out. Pathology is about puzzle solving, and pattern recognition. There's a satisfaction to it. Very cerebral. Very organised. Well, you'd know. You must have become a cyto technician for similar reasons.'

'I became a cyto tech because I'd dropped out of medicine and I was disgusted with myself.' The wine had gone to her head. She shouldn't tell him this stuff. 'I'd planned on being a doctor for so long, but I couldn't juggle it with Josh when he was a baby.'

'Your son? He's—?'

'Eleven. Twelve, soon.'

'OK.' He nodded.

'If I'd been sensible, I would have deferred for a couple of years, but instead I pressed on, took my third-year exams on zero sleep and

failed in spectacular fashion. I guess my—
Realistically, my marriage had already begun
to self-destruct even before he was born and—
Gosh, Verdelho packs a punch, doesn't it?'

'A nice one.' He grinned. His eyes twinkled
and locked her in their beam of dancing Irish
light.

'No, not nice at all,' she said. 'Very tricky.
Because I'm not telling you about my divorce,
I'm telling you about my job. I didn't want to
feel like a complete fai— Well, I wanted to be
connected with medicine in some way—a sat-
isfying way—so I ended up doing a science
degree part time, and then the two-year training course for this full time. I moved back here
about four years ago, and have been peering
down microscopes under Tom Robinson's
guidance ever since.'

'Hmm,' he said. His eyes were still twin-
kling.

'Sorry. I don't usually get tipsy on one glass
of wine, and give people the unexpurgated
story of my life.'

And I don't want you to think I'm this aw-
ful, sozzled divorcee who doesn't know when
to go home.

She stood, and put the empty glass down.

'I topped it up,' he said. 'You didn't notice, I guess.'

'Topped it up? On my empty stomach? You devil.'

'I'm not. But you're right, I should have asked if you wanted it. Innocent mistake. Hey, could you show me that ladder before you go? You said it was in the garage, but I don't re-member seeing it.'

'Oh, Dad's probably got it resting up on the rafters. That's a nuisance. I'll help you get it down. If I can have a very big glass of water first.'

The water helped a bit. They went out to the old-fashioned detached garage, and Declan tackled the big, stiff padlock on the wooden doors with much more authority than Caroline herself could have mustered at the moment. Blame the wine.

He hadn't troubled to put his car inside. Instead, it was sitting on the apron of pale grey concrete in front, a late model Audi, shiny and dark blue.

'Should I keep the car in the garage?' He must have seen her looking at it. 'So far, I've been lazy about it, with no remote-control doors.'

'I don't want to tell you it's safe in the driveway...but I think it probably is, in this street. It's far enough back from the road that it's almost out of sight in the dark.'

Darkness was, in fact, beginning to fall. Maybe she'd been here more than an hour. Declan—he'd said please call him that— swung the doors open and Caroline found the light switch. As a child, she'd considered this garage horribly spooky and still approached it cautiously in case of spiders.

'Yes, it's up there.' She pointed. As well as the ladder, Dad had stored piles of old timber across the rafters, ready for Dad-type carpentry projects which he could only describe in the vaguest terms and which rarely materialised. If he and Mum moved to the Gold Coast permanently after their open-ended trial run, Caroline would have to be very firm with him about getting rid of the wood and not taking it with him. Mum would go nuts.

'How do we get it down?' Declan asked, peering up at the ladder.

'Stand on the workbench. I mean, I will. And I'll pass it to you.'

'No, I'll do it.'

He'd climbed onto the built-in workbench beneath the windows before she could protest. His body moved efficiently, like an athlete's, and the fabric of T-shirt and jeans stretched across his back and thighs. Caroline found herself staring at him, appreciating the male strength, the lack of fuss, the confidence, the whole way he moved. He began to slide the ladder across the beams and she caught her wilful gaze and controlled it just in time.

'It's probably filthy up there,' she told him.

'No! Really?' He lifted his hands, grinned and showed her palms already greyed with dust and grease.

'Oh, worse than I thought! I'm sorry.'

'And me in my best clothes, too. Actually...' He studied her and frowned, his gaze sweeping up and down. She felt herself flushing, self-conscious about the final couple of kilos she still hadn't shed on her diet, the tired blouse she'd been wearing all day and the full breasts beneath, which should belong to some sensual cinematic siren not to a divorcee mother of one in an Australian country town. 'You're the one in the nice clothes.'

'I won't wipe my hands on my skirt.'

'Sure? Because it's about to tip down.' He had the ladder at its balance point on the final beam, and it teetered.

She nodded. 'I'm fine. Sorry about this old garage.'

'I like it, actually. It has character. I can feel it casting its spell. I'm going to start wanting to muck around with tools soon, doing projects.'

Caroline groaned. 'Not you, too!'

'Why, you have a prejudice against home handymen?'

'Home handymen who never finish anything, like my Dad, yes!' Stretching up her hands, she took the ladder and began to ease it to ground level.

Declan jumped down from the bench and came beside her. 'Let me now.'

'All right.'

He stretched in front of her and his shoulder nudged her arm and the side of her breast before she could step back. She caught the warm and oddly pleasing smells of dust, clean cotton and men's anti-perspirant all mingled together, then heard him let out a grunt as he lowered the foot of the ladder to the concrete floor.

'How heavy is it?' she asked, from the safe haven of the driveway in front of his car.

'Not heavy at all.' The ladder's rubber feet scraped across the concrete as he slid it out the garage door, while the top of it cleared the rafters. Then he swung it to the horizontal and carried it back in. He showed no clumsiness, and no apparent effort. 'Here?'

'Yes, if you lay it flat, as I said, the boxes can sit on top, and there should still be room for the car if you do decide to garage it. Do you need help bringing the boxes?'

'No.' He smiled. 'You probably have to—'

'Pick up Josh. Yes.' The excuse she should have used an hour ago, thereby avoiding that lovely, dangerous wine.

'It was good of you to help with the ladder. I'll tell Tom you've made me feel very welcome, very settled,' he drawled, his eyes laughing.

She laughed back at him, still flustered by her reaction to the way his shoulder had felt against her, and by the ease in the way he dealt with her. He acted as if their shared amused embarrassment over dear Tom gave them a sweet secret, as if it had already turned them into friends. While she was relieved at the way this let Tom off the hook, it had begun to disturb her a little, too.

Declan McCulloch was an attractive man. She'd noted that. It was an objective fact. But she couldn't—wouldn't—must not—feel any personal attraction to him herself.

Nice, Declan thought, after she'd gone.

He couldn't get by, in his working environment, without someone to share a laugh with. Tom might never stop trying too hard. Natalia probably had a better sense of humour in her native Russian than she did in English. Secretary Steph and the three lab technicians he hadn't managed to have much of a conversation with today, and had no feeling about yet.

Caroline, on the other hand, seemed intelligent and perceptive and funny, with a solid life of her own beyond the hospital and an odd combination of strength and self-doubt that he liked. An ally, he hoped. Someone to count on.

He made several trips back and forth with flattened boxes then switched off the garage light and closed the creaky doors. His father's car had been garaged behind doors like this— ancient doors, made of splintery wood that didn't get painted often enough, shielding an ancient car, a Morris. It had been held together by sheer Irish bravado and in its final years had been in such bad shape that it had needed to be pushed by Declan and his brothers and sisters almost more than it could be driven.

Good Lord, he was a long way from home!

He hooked the padlock through the catch, then turned towards the house. Darkness had fallen completely by this time, and there was no moon tonight. Despite the light spilling from the windows, the house looked solitary.

Suzy was far away in Sydney.

She kept to an odd timetable with her writing, rising at four and working at her computer through two bowls of cereal and several cups of coffee until around noon. Then she'd eat lunch and take a long nap until four or even five, awaken, shower and be raring to go.

She loved to sit in a restaurant or a bar with a group of friends—other writers, musicians, lawyers, anyone with a dynamic temperament and a quick brain—talking for hours. She'd usually roll into bed at around midnight, sometimes later.

In London, she'd taken him into a world he'd never inhabited before, and he'd enjoyed it enormously. In Sydney, it had been the same. How would they survive the next year, though? Glenfallon was one of those towns mourned in American country music songs, where they rolled up the sidewalks at nine p.m.

Suzy had already told him that her timetable would change once she began working on her novel. She planned to keep more regular hours. But would it be as easy as that? How would she fare, in creative terms, without the urban stimulation she was used to?

Meanwhile, he was alone here, in a town he hadn't heard of this time last year, in a country he'd never planned to come to. It wasn't Suzy's fault. And it wasn't his. They were making the best of the raw material at hand. Suddenly, however, he felt lonely, and not fully convinced that the loneliness would disappear if Suzy herself appeared magically at the front door.

CHAPTER FOUR

'HAS he said when Suzy will be down?' Tom asked.

'No, he's said he doesn't know yet when she'll be down, because it'll depend on re-writes.'

'I wish she'd already finished the TV thing and was ready to start the novel.'

'I think she's ready personally, it's the contractual commitment to the TV series that's the problem. They're running behind schedule, apparently.'

'Because I'm really keen to organise this barbecue while the weather's still nice. You know, showcase our wonderful outdoor life-style.'

'Is Eileen in Melbourne at the moment, then, Tom?' Caroline asked gently.

He blinked. 'Yes. She went yesterday. How did you know?'

'Oh, the aura of quiet desperation and imminent emotional breakdown might have given me a small clue.'

'That bad?'

'Believe it! Look, he invited me in for a glass of wine the other night...'

'That's great! You didn't tell me!'

No, I kept it to myself, and I'm still not sure why.

'And we had a bit of a heart-to-heart.'

'Even better! If he feels he has friends here in the department...'

'And as I guessed before, it's just not going to happen, what you're hoping for. He considered himself settled in London before he met Suzy. He was prepared to move to Sydney for her sake, and to suffer through this rural exile for a year, at most two, but they're both city-oriented—'

'She wants to bury herself in the bush to wrestle with her great *oeuvre*.'

'Only until it's finished. Then, from what he said, his time here will be up and she very clearly sees herself landing back in Sydney with a splash upon the novel's publication, ready to be the toast of the town.'

'She's confident!'

'Yes, I got that impression. Confident and urban.'

'We'll still do the barbecue.'

'Of course. But no big, throbbing hidden agenda with it, Tom, really. And if she's not available for a couple more weeks, the delay doesn't matter.'

'No, damn it.' He beat his fist in his palm. 'We'll have it this weekend. Without her. He shouldn't be condemned to solitary misery just because she's not here. Natalia wants it this weekend.'

Everyone wanted it this weekend. Declan himself seemed happy to go along with the plan. Tom asked the rest of the department to invite a few friends who might be likely to become bosom buddies with the new arrival. Since Caroline thought it wise to dilute the atmosphere as much as possible, she co-opted her old friends Emma and Nell, newer friend Kit, and Kit's and Emma's husbands, Gian and Pete.

Natalia and Alexei Akmanov were not fans of gardening. They'd recently put in an in-ground, solar-heated and gorgeously land-scaped pool which, along with de luxe barbe-cue and jarrahwood outdoor furniture, filled their entire back yard.

It was the perfect setting for a gathering of this kind. Everyone brought swim gear, drinks and a contribution to the meal. There must have been at least forty people present, including Declan himself, by the time Caroline arrived.

He stood by the barbecue, talking to Alexei, Gian, Pete and a man Caroline didn't know, which left Caroline's three friends free to huddle with her near the drinks table and ask questions.

'He looks nice,' Emma said. 'Is he?'

'So far. Hasn't blamed the cyto techs for any of his own mistakes yet.'

'Ouch!' Kit said. 'I just had a Pap test on Friday. How many mistakes has he made?'

'None, I hope! No, I just meant he doesn't seem the type to use medical hierarchy to his own advantage. You're nurses, Kit, Emma, you know what I mean.'

'Where's the girlfriend?'

'Yes, I want to meet Suzy Screenwriter.' Nell gave her wicked, cynical grin.

'I should never have said that to you, Nell!'

'I like it.'

'You would!'

'She's not standing with him, though,' Kit observed. 'Is she—?'

'In Sydney. Not here. Tom got stubborn and decided not to wait till she was free.'

'He doesn't look as if he minds. Declan, that is.'

'Oh, I'm sure he does, though. He's not the kind of man who'd show it, do you think?'

'We don't know him, Caroline,' Emma reminded her. 'You do.'

'Not well, after a week.'

He glanced across and saw her at that moment, lifted his glass and smiled. She waved back, and felt a sudden sensation of warmth and happiness that she knew was dangerous. She *didn't* know him, she reminded herself. Not really.

And she did know that he was emotionally involved elsewhere. Yet there was a curling tendril of awareness in her that seemed to grow each time she saw him, and that she couldn't control.

'Kit, Bonnie's not with you today?' she asked Kit Di Luzio quickly, as a way of deflecting attention from the new man in town.

'No, Freddie has her. Gian and I knew we wouldn't have a second's peace with her around the pool. She's so confident. I could see her launching herself into the water when we weren't looking, and forgetting completely that she can't swim.'

Kit and Gian had formally adopted three-year-old Bonnie last year. She was Gian's brother's child, legacy of a short-lived relationship. Marco Di Luzio hadn't even known about Bonnie until her mother's death when Bonnie had been just a few months old.

Caroline knew that Kit and Gian would like to have a child of their own, too, but Kit had struggled with infertility in a previous relationship, so no one ever teased her or Gian about baby-making as they might have done with another newly married couple.

Emma and Pete were only recently married, too. Three weeks ago, in fact, after a very cautious courtship and engagement. Pete had had a lot of problems to sort out with his ex-wife, and both he and Emma's priority had been to make sure his little twin daughters felt settled and secure.

'Jessie and Zoe are swimming like tadpoles, Emma,' Nell commented, watching Emma's new stepdaughters.

'I know. Aren't they gorgeous?'

'Barbecue's ready, everyone,' Pete said. He came up and touched Emma on the arm. 'We'd better get the girls out of the pool.'

Still thinking about her friends' weddings, Caroline stayed by the drinks table, sipping her wine spritzer, while the others dissipated in the direction of pool or barbecue.

She had cried luxuriously on both occasions. She always cried at weddings, and had decided that attempting not to cry only made her worse. It did her good, somehow, to witness the right two people joining themselves in marriage, to remind herself that there were men in the world who weren't like Robert.

Robert had phoned a couple of days ago. He wanted to take Josh for a weekend in Sydney, soon. There was a father-and-son rugby coaching clinic coming up at Woodside. Last year, he'd wrestled a reluctant agreement from her that Josh would drop that silly soccer stuff when he reached high school and play Robert's old game of rugby union instead. Given this agreement, it was understandable that Robert wanted Josh to get a head start with the game.

Why at Woodside, though?

It was Robert's old school. They'd put Josh's name down there as a baby, but surely Robert wouldn't expect him to attend now. There was a good private boys' school here in Glenfallon which should answer any of Robert's arguments about the importance of plugging their son into the right old boys' network.

If Josh went to Woodside, he'd have to go as a boarder, and that would mean—

'Not hungry?' Declan asked her. She hadn't even noticed his approach.

'Hungry but not pushy,' she answered. 'Happy to wait.'

'You were frowning. I wondered if something was wrong.'

'I'm fine.' She smiled, then made a point of inhaling the aromas rising from his filled plate. 'And looking at that lot—emphasis on *lot*— I'm getting hungrier by the second.'

'Now, if that's a more-than-broad hint that I've taken more than my share, Caroline Archer...'

'What would have given you that idea?' She felt comfortable teasing Declan, after what he'd said on Monday evening—that Tom's innocent pressure would be easier to take if he had someone to laugh with.

'Australians are pretty good at food,' Declan said. 'Especially outdoor food. And they're not afraid of an ethnic mix, I've noticed. English sausages, Middle Eastern kebabs, Indonesian satay sticks, Russian piroshki… I felt that as the supposed guest of honour it would be only tactful of me to sample everything, so as not to unwittingly offend.'

'You're making that up on the spot.'

'Ah, you're right. It's pure greed, actually.'

The only problem was that between a man and a woman teasing was a cousin to flirting, and she knew she could too easily forget the difference. Her gaze drifted from his heaped plate and snagged on his forearm, where the sun glinted on a soft shading of dark gold hair. He wore baggy, sand-coloured shorts that reached to his knees and an open-topped shirt.

He had a lovely neck.

A lot of men didn't. Too thick, or too short. And a lot of women didn't seem to consider necks. They fixated on pecs, biceps, butts and thighs. However, necks were close to the top of Caroline's list—lean, smooth, lightly tanned necks, not too long and not too short, curving out into straight shoulders below and a clear jawline above.

Back off, she told herself. Keep the boundaries in place.

But she couldn't make the boundaries too high and strong, or Tom would think she was letting him and Eileen down. It was a fine line to tread.

'Hey, I'm playing tennis next weekend,' Declan told her. 'With a couple of doctors I've only just met and the husband of the pathology department secretary's sister. Any idea what that's about? Nothing to do with Tom, I don't suppose?'

'Oh, Declan!'

'It's all right. I like tennis. Although I'll have to surreptitiously whack balls against the side of your dad's garage all week to get up my match-winning form.'

She laughed and, as if getting this reaction had been his only goal in approaching her in the first place, he dismissed her immediately afterwards with a light command. 'Go on, get some food before it all disappears.'

When she'd done so, she took care to wander off in another direction, and barely exchanged another word with him for the rest of the afternoon. She noted, though, that he spread his attention very evenly between all the guests who'd been invited to meet him, and that reassured her.

He hadn't flirted with her. He was only being polite.

'Caroline, I've just been called down to A and E for a fine needle aspiration,' Declan said.

'Oh, yes?' Caroline looked up from the slide she was screening.

He stood in the doorway of the cyto techs' office, looking relaxed and cheerful. Was Suzy coming down this weekend? she wondered. Not everyone managed to look relaxed and cheerful this late on a Friday, so it could well be that he had something in particular to look forward to—something which stripped away the end-of-week fatigue that everyone else struggled with. Half an hour ago, for example, she'd heard a crash of metal and glass and some very frustrated swearing issuing from the lab along the corridor.

'Want to come and prep the slides for me?' he said. 'This is my first trip down there, and things might be different to what I'm used to.'

'No problem.' She took a quick look at her watch and saw it was already nearly four-thirty. Not the usual time for a FNA, especially on a Friday. It must be urgent.

They threaded their way together through a series of stairs, internal corridors and walk-ways, collecting the relevant trolley from the storage room near Outpatients on their way through. Nell encountered them as they arrived in her department.

'The fine needle?' she said. 'Patient in Room Three?'

'You've seen her?' Declan asked.

Nell nodded tightly. 'Get a sample if you can,' she said. 'If you can't...' She let her words trail off, and disappeared into another room.

Declan shrugged at Caroline, and she clicked her tongue in reply. Nell was rarely very communicative on the job. As for herself and Declan, they weren't all that communica-tive either, but somehow it felt different. A shrug and the click of a tongue could speak volumes with the right person, she'd found.

What had Nell meant by suggesting Declan might not get a sample?

The patient in Room Three, Alison Scanlon, was just shy of her fortieth birthday, according to the new file just created for her. No previous medical history of relevance. She'd presented in the emergency department half an hour ago, with bleeding just below her armpit.

The bleeding 'wouldn't seem to stop', she'd said. Now she sat rigidly upright on the edge of the treatment table, pressing a gauze pad to the side of her right breast. She'd been crying, and so had the woman with her—her sister, if family resemblance was any guide. They both had dark blonde hair, small, uptilted noses and freckles on fair skin.

The emotion in the room was palpable—anger as well as tears. The sister glared at Alison, her lips pressed shut, her jaw shaking, her eyes red and swollen. Alison didn't look at her. Staring stony-eyed into the air, she seemed locked in her own private hell, and Caroline felt the hairs on the back of her neck stand on end.

Declan must have noticed the atmosphere, but this didn't show from his manner.

'I'm Dr McCulloch,' he said. 'And this is my technician, Caroline. We're going to be drawing some material from your breast. Your right breast, isn't it?'

'She won't let me see it,' the sister said. 'She wouldn't show me, but I made her come in.'

'You bullied me, Megan.'

'Don't you dare tell me that!'

'It sounds as if you've done the right thing to seek some help,' Declan assured both women in a neutral tone. 'Can we get you to lie down, Alison? This won't take long.'

Although at this rate, the seconds would stretch. A fine needle aspiration wasn't usually this tense.

Caroline checked her trolley. Slides, fixative, staining solutions, rinser, all present and correct. Declan would need syringe and needle first. She put on gloves and took the items from a drawer to hand to him.

Alison had tears rolling down her cheeks again. Although she'd lain down as Declan had asked, she still had the gauze pressed to her breast. 'We'll need you to lie flat now, and to take your hand away,' he told her.

She gave a sharp little nod, closed her eyes, tightened her mouth into a creased slit and carefully lifted her hand and the blood-soaked gauze pad from her breast. Looking up from her trolley, Caroline felt ill at what she saw, and Megan gasped and swore and almost screamed.

'My God, Alison, my God, my God!'

'Leave me alone, OK?'

Declan somehow managed not to betray the horror they all felt. This woman had a lump on her breast the size and consistency of an overripe plum. It was weepy and boggy and bleeding, and the patient must have known for months that something was seriously wrong.

'Why did you let this happen?' her sister said on a harsh whisper. 'My God, I used to be a nurse. If you'd shown me... Why?'

'How do I know why? It got away from me. It didn't seem to matter. After the divorce...'

'Is Eddie the only person who counts? And the fact that he left? I am so angry with you! I am so unspeakably angry! What about the rest of us? How dare you hurt Mum and Dad, and me and Lukey and *everyone* by letting this happen, Alison?'

'Alison,' Declan's voice came in quietly. 'I need you to lie still for me now so I can see if we've any chance of getting a sample. Caroline, can you pass me a fresh dressing?

I'm going to see if I can clean the skin around the area. And, Alison, I'm going to have a little press, here, to see what's going on.'

He did his best, palpating the distended side of the breast in search of a distinct tumour, but Caroline wasn't at all surprised when he announced, after a minute or two, 'No, we're not going to go ahead with the procedure, Alison.'

'What does that mean?' she rasped out. 'Are you sending me home?'

He broke the thick silence after just a second or two. 'No, I'm not sending you home. Not for long, anyway. I'm sending you—' He broke off. 'Forgive me, I'm new around here. Where are we sending her, Caroline?'

'Canberra. Dr Cassidy will want to send her to Canberra.'

'Of course. To Canberra. You'll be referred to an oncologist there, who will decide on the best course of treatment. You'll most likely receive a course of radio-and chemotherapy to try and shrink the mass before surgery. It'll take around six weeks, on an outpatient basis. You'll be able to talk to someone here about how to arrange accommodation near the hospital.'

He raised his eyebrows at Caroline and she confirmed with a quick nod that, yes, that was the way it would work here.

'So it's c-cancer?' Alison's jaw shuddered.

'I'm sorry, Alison. It's a sizeable malignant mass. There's no point in my trying to soften the news.'

'How can you even ask him that?' Megan cut in, almost yelling at her sister. '*Now* you ask? *Now* you act like this is a shock?'

Alison closed her eyes again and a fresh brimming of tears squeezed out. 'I know it doesn't make sense. I know I've been stupid. Which doesn't make it easier, Megan, believe me. Knowing I should have done something about it. Showed you. Believe me, it doesn't make it any easier.'

'Listen, we'll do everything we can, OK?' Megan's voice came on a harsh whisper, cracking with every second word. 'I'll come to Canberra with you, at least for the first couple of treatments. We can beat this. It may not have spread.'

Caroline and Declan left the sisters still talking in a whirl of dark emotion. The squeaking wheel of the trolley provided an incongruous note of banality as Caroline nudged it through the doorway to return it to where it lived.

'Is there any chance she can beat it?' she murmured to Declan as they headed for the nurses' station to speak to Nell.

He shook his head slowly. 'I wouldn't be very optimistic. A mass that size. It has to have spread elsewhere. They'll scan her for secondaries in Canberra, of course. It was granulated, inflamed...'

'Carcinoma. Why did she let it happen? I understand exactly how her sister feels! There are obviously people who care about her who are going to be devastated by this.'

'She's devastated now, herself, I think.'

'Then why?'

'People play games with themselves, Caroline. They stick their tongues out at death and fate and love. Her self-esteem was obviously low after the divorce.'

'And the lump grew one day at a time, I guess. There was always tomorrow. It wouldn't be that much worse, she probably thought, if she did something about it tomorrow, and not today.'

'Exactly. Too many tomorrows, coming one at a time. Well, we're just philosophising here, psychoanalysing. It's bewildering. That's one of the more extreme cases of denial that I've seen.'

Nell looked up from the notes she was scribbling. 'Could you do anything with it?'

Declan shook his head. 'There's no palpable tumour, nowhere to stick the needle even if there'd been a hope of getting an uncontaminated sample.'

'So, Canberra.'

'So Caroline tells me.'

'Radio, chemo, then back here for a biopsy, to see exactly what we're dealing with. Her odds aren't good, are they?'

'No, and she knows it.'

'Did the sister see it?'

'Yes.'

'Alison wouldn't let her in before. I nearly gasped out loud, when I got her to show me.' Nell shook her head, and though the movement was as brisk and cool as usual, Caroline could tell that her old friend had reacted the same way she had herself.

'The sister screamed,' Declan said. 'I got the feeling it might do Alison good to find out how much her family cares.'

'There are better ways to find out that people care,' Nell said.

She was right, and after that statement there didn't seem to be anything more left to say. Caroline and Declan headed along the walkway toward the other building, and neither of them spoke until they'd reached the stairs. Steph came past, on her way out, and wished them both a nice weekend. Caroline's reply came out stiltedly, but Steph was in too much of a hurry to notice. She had car keys already jingling in her hand.

'Are you all right now, Caroline?' Declan asked.

'I'm fine. I'll go home to Josh and give him a big hug.'

'He's a nice kid, I bet.' Although it was just a polite line, he sounded as if he meant it. Caroline couldn't help checking his face with a quick, covert glance. She knew she'd begun to look at him too often…though not as often as she wanted to.

'Well, I think so,' she answered, looking away again. 'But mothers aren't very objective. What about you, Declan? Is Suzy coming down this weekend? I hope you're not going home to an empty house.'

'She's still in Sydney.'

'Oh. That's a pity.'

She almost blurted out an invitation.

Come home and have dinner with Josh and me.

She could almost believe that he wanted her to. He'd stopped, just in front of the door that led into the department, as if he was waiting. He had a smile on his face. Barely there, really. Just a tiny upward flick at the corners, and a softening around his unlined eyes. Warmth flooded her.

She took in a breath. 'Well,' she said. 'I'll tidy my desk.'

'Mmm. Is the House of Siam any good, do you know?'

'I've had take-away from there, with Josh, and we liked it. But we're both good with spicy food.'

'Whereas Irishmen only like stew and potatoes?' Now he was really smiling, teasing her for her unthinking reliance on stereotypes.

'Sorry!' she said.

He clicked his tongue. 'I'll see you on Monday, Caroline.'

* * *

'Mmm,' Emma said. 'Can I go to sleep now?'

'No,' Kit answered, merciless. 'I want my turn.'

'Same here,' Caroline agreed.

'I now realise,' Nell mumbled, 'that having first turn was a mistake.'

'What does the book say?'

'"Draw the massage peacefully to a close, on an outward breath",' Caroline read. '"Gently cover the patient with a warmed towel. Invite him/her to rest for a few minutes before rising from the massage table." Reading between the lines, and leaving out the fact that we're not using massage tables, I interpret that to mean you're not allowed to go to sleep.'

'Wait till you're in our position!' Nell mumbled again.

Nell was the one who'd bought the teach-yourself-massage book and suggested that it would be a fun thing to do together over the course of several weekends. This sort of thing had become a keynote to the friendship between the four women over the past year. They'd actively challenged the notion that for single women there was 'nothing to do' in an Australian country town of Glenfallon's size by generating their own entertainment.

Last year's winery tour had been the first item in their informal programme. Emma had given them several French cooking lessons following a three-month break from nursing spent at an *école de cuisine* in Paris. Kit was researching setting up a book group under the auspices of the local library.

Caroline thought they ought to do more with movies than simply each rent something separately from the video shop at the last minute on a Sunday evening and take it home to watch in solitary state at home.

Of course, Kit and Emma weren't solitary any more. They each had a lovely man to snuggle up with in front of their movies.

Caroline knew Nell well enough to perceive that beneath her often caustic exterior she was frightened about this—frightened of being the last one left, of losing all her female friends to widened horizons and changed lives.

I don't think she has too much to worry about in my case, Caroline thought as she stripped to the waist and lay face down on the towel-covered camping sleep-mat on Emma's living-room floor. She adjusted a couple of rolled up towels against her torso so that they accommodated the press of her breasts, and was comfortable.

And marriage hadn't taken Kit and Emma away, in any case, her train of thought continued. Or not yet. They'd loved the massage idea.

Gian and Pete weren't around this afternoon. They'd been co-opted into Tom's social men's tennis programme with poor Declan. Bonnie was with her grandmother, and Pete's girls had gone to Canberra for the weekend to spend some time with his ex-wife, Claire. With the house all to themselves, it was very pleasant to have soft music in the background while they went through the book's step-by-step instructions on how to massage the back, shoulders and spine.

Caroline abandoned herself to the relaxing sensations and soon understood exactly why Nell and Emma had pleaded so shamelessly for sleep. Time stopped. She hardly heard the music. Didn't think about her worries concerning Robert and Josh. Didn't think about anything. She just relaxed...

'"Stroke firmly outwards with both hands from the base of the spine to the hips, then recommence the effleurage movement at the shoulders''.' Emma had a soothing, musical voice as she read each instruction aloud to Nell.

'It's a bloody nuisance.' Feet drummed without warning on the wooden floorboards of the veranda at the front of the house. Their rhythm was irregular, and unmistakably male. Caroline had only vaguely heard a car somewhere close. A groan sounded. 'I hope I can drive tomorrow, or Emma's going to have to ferry me to and fro. Thanks for doing this, Declan.'

That was Pete's voice. They weren't supposed to finish their tennis this early. And apparently Declan was with him. 'It's only a few streets out of my way,' he said.

Caroline heard Pete's key rattle in the lock and both men entered. Without opening her eyes, Caroline could hear that one of them was hobbling. Pete, apparently.

Emma's hands stilled on Caroline's shoulder blades. Her sensitised skin could feel the slippery film of massage oil between her back and Emma's fingers, and the lavender and rosemary essences in the oil rose strong and spicy-sweet to her nostrils.

'Sprained my damned ankle, Emma,' Pete said in the doorway. 'Oops.'

'Oops' was right, Declan thought, beside him.

The scene that greeted the two men was very innocent, yet somehow very private. He'd met Pete and the others at the tennis club, and hadn't known that at home Emma would have company. Or a class, or whatever it was. A massage class, apparently. He'd heard Emma's voice, through the open living-room window, reading out something about effleurage, just before Pete hobbled onto the veranda.

That was Caroline Archer in the middle of the floor, and Nell Cassidy, head of Glenfallon Hospital's emergency department, bending over another female body which he didn't want to look at any more closely in its current state of undress.

Anyway, it was Caroline who drew his attention.

She'd swept her loose dark hair up from her neck so that it didn't get caught in the massage oil. Tendrils of hair streaked across her face and onto the rolled towel that supported her cheek, creating a strong contrast of colour and making her look as if she'd fallen asleep after some wild session of love-making. Her eyes were closed, and the planes of her face looked still and relaxed.

Her arms lay at her sides, bent slightly outward. Her fingers were curled and soft, and her skin looked as tender as a baby's. Her back glistened with oil, from her shoulders all the way down her spine. A towel was draped over her legs, reaching almost to her hips and exposing the stretch of skin where her buttocks began to swell.

'We'll leave you to it,' Pete concluded. 'Beer, Declan? Out the back, I think.'

'That'd be great,' Declan answered.

And quickly, please, he added to himself, before anyone realises that I was staring, and that there's a tightness across the front of my shorts that shouldn't be there.

He stepped back from the doorway and offered his shoulder for Pete to lean on as he hobbled along the corridor towards the back of the house. Pete passed him two cans of beer from the fridge, grabbed a packet of frozen peas for his ankle and they manoeuvred their way to the shady back veranda. Declan sank into a wooden outdoor chair with a groan of relief, just as Pete did, but for different reasons.

Sure, what he'd just experienced had been a normal, physical, male reaction that no man ever expected to be able to fully control. It came, and it passed, and it wasn't a problem…except when a man hadn't seen his girlfriend for two weeks and wouldn't be seeing her for at least five days more.

In such a situation as that, it…no, still wasn't a problem. The reaction had subsided now, and he hadn't the remotest intention of acting on it, or reading more into it than simple male physiology.

But it was annoying.

He hadn't expected so much vagueness and uncertainty from Suzy as to when she'd be able to get down here. Before he'd moved from Sydney, she'd spoken blithely about commuting up from Glenfallon for script meetings and doing most of her actual writing here.

So far, that hadn't happened.

Apparently she needed to consult more closely and more frequently with script editors and other writers than she'd anticipated. Her episodes were set in Sydney, too, and she needed to visit some of the locations in order to accurately envisage certain scenes.

That made sense.

Declan supported her career, and understood it as far as Suzy was able to explain it to him. But he liked to be able to make plans. He'd had a chaotic childhood, full of unpredictable streaks of hard times and equally unpredictable spells of good fortune, with an ongoing sense that you never knew which way the financial wind would blow next.

Would Mum have a job? Would Dad win on the horses? Would they be celebrating this time next week? Or scraping the mould off the bread and hiding the dodgy taste and stale texture of it beneath a puddle of cheap jam?

Was Suzy coming down at the end of the week, or not?

If so, he could relax a bit. If not, he wanted to know as soon as possible, so he could get used to the idea.

She didn't seem to understand any of this. 'I'll let you know,' she'd said last night, when he'd talked to her on the phone.

'When?'

'Well, before I get in the car, Dec, OK? Is that good enough?'

'Sure. It's fine. Whatever you can manage.'

He drank his beer quickly. Pete looked grumpy and restless, and kept glancing back into the house, obviously hoping that the massage session would finish soon so that he and Emma could be alone. Declan understood exactly how he felt.

'Will you be all right now?' he asked Pete, after downing the last third of the can in one draught.

'Emma will look after me.' Pete frowned at the ankle, which he'd raised onto the cushioned seat of the adjacent chair and draped in its plastic packet of peas. 'As long as I stay off it today, I'm hoping it'll be all right tomorrow.'

'You had three doctors poking at it, including yourself, and none of us thought it was serious.' He stood up. 'I'll be heading off home, I think.'

'Thanks for driving me.'

'Thanks for the beer.'

'No problem, Declan.'

From her prone position, Caroline heard Declan's footsteps striding down the corridor. 'I'll let myself out, Emma,' he said in the doorway, and then the front door opened and shut at once, and he thudded across the veranda and down the steps. His car started up less than a minute later.

'Your shoulders feel very tight,' Emma told her.

'Sorry.'

'No, I meant, am I not doing it right? You felt good and relaxed before the men came back early.'

'Pete probably wants us to leave.'

'Don't worry about it. We're up to the last series of movements now. It won't be long.'

Caroline and Kit lay there as Nell and Emma had done, but Caroline wasn't tempted by sleep. The massage had been ruined for her as soon as she'd heard Declan's voice. She'd kept her eyes closed, but hadn't needed to look towards the doorway to realise that he'd have seen her naked, glistening back. He probably hadn't bothered to look at it for more than a second, but still she'd felt vulnerable.

And foolish, somehow. She hadn't wanted a near-stranger and new colleague to see her and her friends bumbling through their self-taught massage programme. It was a girl thing.

'Now, as the book says, you should rest there for a few minutes before you try to move,' Emma instructed both her and Kit. 'No, don't pack up the oil and the spare towels, Nell. I'll do it.'

She jumped up and went down the corridor to Pete. Nell disappeared into the bathroom, and half a minute later Caroline and Kit both heard Emma helping Pete to hobble back into the house. They heard snatches of their conversation as well.

'We were going to go out to dinner tonight,' Pete was saying.

'We can still do that. I'll drive.'

'I never wanted to play tennis in the first place.' The fridge door opened and closed, and kitchen sounds began to mask some of their words. 'Tom's campaign...' Caroline heard, and 'our precious time alone....'

Emma's voice dropped to a soothing murmur, then there was silence and private laughter.

'We'd better go,' Kit said. 'I wonder if Gian's still playing, or if he's already at home. I don't know how many other players they had.'

She sat up, wrapped a towel around her back, dried off the oil and reached for her clothing. In a hurry to give Emma and Pete their privacy, Caroline wondered, or to get home to her own man? Probably both.

I'll pick Josh up from Rohan's early, she decided. He won't want to come yet, but that's tough.

She put on her blouse and found her watch. Four o'clock. Josh had been at his friend's since ten. He couldn't complain. They'd make pizza together and negotiate on the rental of a video they'd both enjoy. It would be fun.

She hoped he wouldn't ask about having a sleep-over. She didn't feel she saw enough of him as it was, and next weekend the threatened rugby coaching clinic was happening, so she wouldn't see him at all.

Robert had sent a plane ticket for him. Josh had a terrible time with the small propeller-driven aircraft that flew between Sydney and Glenfallon. Even with a motion sickness pill, it would be touch and go, and if Robert and Josh forgot about him taking the pill well in advance for the flight home, as was quite likely...

Josh would have had a much easier journey on the train, or by car. Six hours' drive was such an awkward distance away. Close enough that weekends weren't completely out of the question, but too far to make it an easy trip, and the plane and train services weren't frequent enough. Was that why Declan was alone again this weekend?

When she got to Rohan's, both boys besieged her with pleas for a sleep-over, just as she'd feared. Rohan's mum, who was a nice woman, told her with a helpless shrug, 'I've said yes, as long as it's all right with you.'

Caroline didn't have the heart to refuse, so she made eggs for herself instead of pizza that night, rented a movie that Josh would have hated, and couldn't help thinking, more than once, as she pottered around her too-quiet house, Declan McCulloch is alone this weekend, too. I wonder what he's doing with himself tonight?

CHAPTER FIVE

CAROLINE looked at the pile of slide trays in Julianne's arms and knew she'd be staying late today. Her in-tray, which would usually have been empty at this stage of the afternoon, had several wooden and cardboard racks still awaiting her attention. She hadn't worked with her usual concentration.

'Now?' she said to the lab technician. She softened her exasperated tone with a smile. 'You bring me this lot now, at four on a Monday afternoon?'

'They're mostly Paps. Just a couple of other things. You can leave them till tomorrow.'

'By which time you'll have another pile for me, right?'

'Right, but you'll have Natalia to help.'

'Not good enough. I'll at least make a start this afternoon.' Or get rid of as much of the old pile as she could. Ten cases, say. That was a nice, round number.

She reached for the phone and dialled her neighbour, who had teenagers and was always happy to have Josh over for an hour or so when necessary. Then she phoned Josh himself, to warn him not to expect her until six-ish and suggest that he pop next door. Mrs Hollis was expecting him, and Steve Hollis had just received a new video game system for his birthday. Further inducement was not required.

She hoped his energy levels would hold up, though. His flight had been late in from Sydney last night, and he'd been so nauseous that they'd had to sit in Glenfallon's tiny terminal for half an hour before he'd been able to face the car journey home.

'Didn't Dad give you the motion sickness tablet?'

'He forgot.'

'Why didn't you remind him?'

'I forgot, too.'

She'd had to give him a late meal, and it had been after ten by the time he'd got to bed.

He hadn't said much about the weekend. Just a gruff, 'It was OK,' which could have meant anything. Interpreting body language rather than words, she was pretty sure he hadn't enjoyed it much. No surprise there. She didn't think he was made for rugby, either physically or mentally, and wondered how long it would be before Robert would see this himself and let go of the idea.

Am I handling Robert the right way? she wondered.

He'd remarried four years ago, and he and Gail had a little daughter, aged thirteen months. He doted on Amelia, naturally. Caroline would have doted on a darling baby daughter, too! And it wasn't fair to say that Amelia had pushed Josh aside in Robert's heart, but all the same...

He seemed to make these authoritative pronouncements on Josh's future without taking the time to think about who Josh was, or consider alternatives. Josh would attend Woodside. Josh would play rugby. Josh should aim for medicine or law. Orthopaedic surgery would be an excellent choice, following in Robert's own footsteps.

And last night, when Caroline had phoned to confirm their son's safe arrival home, Robert had casually told her, 'He'll have to come up again in three weeks. Woodside is having its academic testing for next year's year sevens and a tour of the school.'

'Three weeks?'

'I know, it's a bit much so soon, but it can't be helped. I'm sorry we both forgot the motion sickness stuff. I must ask Gail to stay on top of things like that with him. She's so much better at that sort of detail than I am.'

'I'll drive him up,' she'd said. 'I won't put him on the plane again. I'd like to see the school, too. I'm sure the facilities at Woodside can't be so very superior to what Ranleigh has to—'

But Robert never wanted to consider Ranleigh. 'It'd be great if you'd drive up, yes. You'll be impressed with Woodside, I promise. You know I'm prepared to pay the full cost of tuition and boarding, so there's really no disincentive for you.'

Yes, there was.

But she didn't go through the argument again.

Instead, she just slept badly, and couldn't focus at work, so now she was behind.

Taking a deep breath, she slid another piece of rectangular glass beneath her microscope lens and began to examine the clusters of cells. By the time she got to the sixth case of the ten more she'd promised herself she'd get through, she was so tired that she'd already revised her promise downward to eight. Or seven, if this dawning headache got worse.

It took her several seconds, too, to realise that the name on the slide was familiar.

Sandie McLennan.

Her brother Chris's wife.

And this wasn't a routine Pap smear, it was a fine needle aspiration that Declan or Tom must have done this morning here at the hospital. She brought up the information already logged into the computer. Yes, Declan had done it, and the name was no coincidence. All the other details fitted her sister-in-law, too.

OK, she reassured herself. The problem wasn't necessarily serious. Surely Sandie would have said something if she was worried about her health in any way.

Caroline snapped the first slide onto the microscope platform. It made its usual glassy *tink* sound, then squeaked as she slid it into position. The department was very quiet. The lab techs had gone home, and so had Steph. Declan and Tom might still be around, or they might have left, too. All she could hear was the faint hum of the computer, irritating rather than soothing at this hour.

She flicked the knob around to focus the slide, then searched for a good grouping of cells within the pretty stainings of pink and purple. Owl eyes stared back at her, too many pairs of them to count.

Owl eyes!

She went cold, and her heart began to pound in her chest. She hadn't wanted to see something like this. Arranged randomly amongst the normal lymphocyte cells, each abnormal cell was much larger, and contained two nuclei instead of one. This was the 'owl eyes' effect that had struck her so forcefully at once. Within each nucleus was a smaller circle that stained redder with the dye the lab technicians used. This was another indicator that the cells were abnormal.

Abnormal, and easily recognised, to her trained eye.

Hodgkin's cells.

Cancer cells.

There were five slides in Sandie's sample, and all of them looked the same. Forcing herself to stay calm, Caroline went through each one. These weren't cross-sections of tissue. There was no 'architecture', as doctors called it. The sample had been centrifuged in a special machine to concentrate the cells and separate them from the fluid, then dyed and smeared onto the slides. In a case like this, there was no possibility of error.

Those large, owl-eyed cells denoted Hodgkin's lymphoma.

Sandie had cancer.

Caroline gulped back a hiccuping sob of shock. She pushed her chair back and fled her microscope and her office, holding the last of Sandie's slides between one forefinger and thumb. The edges of the glass could have cut her if she'd gripped it any harder.

Questions hammered in her mind. Regret and guilt washed back and forth. She paced the corridor, thinking, I should pack up, turn off the equipment. I'm not going to get those other cases done. I should go home to Josh. But if he sees I'm upset, and wants to know what's wrong...

She hadn't realised that Declan was still there until she heard a sound and saw him appear around the corner of the corridor, his stride long and easy, his smile already in place. 'Thought everyone had gone,' he said, then took a better look at her face. 'Hey...'

She tried to smile. 'Yes, I'm a sight, aren't I?'

'You're upset,' he corrected, not fooled. 'What's wrong?'

'I— Nothing. I...' She only realised then that she still had the slide in her fingers.

'Don't tell me... You haven't made a mistake, and Tom hasn't yelled at you, so...' He looked at the rectangle of glass in her hand. 'This is something serious?' He looked more closely at her face. 'Yes, and it's someone you know.'

'Should I tell you?' She waved the slide in her frantic hand. 'It's confidential. I'm caught in this cleft stick of—'

'I'll be looking at it in any case, won't I, to sign off on the diagnosis?'

'Yes. Of course you will. I'm not thinking at all. You already have. You did the fine needle aspiration this morning.' The realisation focused her fracturing awareness a little. She took a breath. 'This is my sister-in-law,' she explained. 'My brother's wife. We're quite close. We should be closer, only I haven't made the effort to go out to their property as often as I should lately.'

'She didn't tell you about this? What is it?'

'Hodgkin's lymphoma, unmistakable in every slide. I'm wondering if she knows. If her GP indicated his real level of concern. She must have had symptoms.'

'Fatigue, weight loss, night sweats, aching joints, loss of appetite. You'd think so, yes. People often put those symptoms down to something else, though. Stress. Flu.'

'Stress! As if there's any farmer in this state who hasn't been stressed, these past couple of years, with the drought! I might have realised it was more than that, if she'd told me about the way she'd been feeling. She might have gone to her doctor sooner if I'd been there to give her some encouragement.'

Caroline began to shake and she felt nauseous. She hugged her arms around herself, fighting both sensations. Sandie and Chris's two boys were still so young, just four and seven. Sandie would be in anguish at the thought that cancer might take her from them, and from the husband she loved.

Declan stood there, and Caroline whispered an apology, thinking that he must hate this, must wish he'd left ten minutes ago. He reached out and put a hand on her shoulder, but he must have felt the gesture to be inadequate—and it was—because a moment later he stepped forward and took her into his arms.

'Hey…' he said again, like soothing a baby, or a foal.

He stroked a hand up and down her back, patted the back of her head, made sh-sh sounds in his Irish accent. She rested her forehead on his shoulder, where firm, elastic muscle softened the straight, sturdy ridge of bone.

His pale shirt smelled of apple-scented laundry detergent and sunny air, and the crook of his arm around her warmed her side and her back. He felt big against her body, strong, sure of himself and of the comfort he offered her. For herself, she could have drowned in it. She'd never been in his arms before, and yet it felt familiar, as if she belonged. At any other time, she would have fought the feeling, but right now she couldn't.

'This isn't your fault, Caroline,' he said. 'You can beat yourself up over not going to visit your family often enough if you want, but don't blame yourself for a twist of fate that's out of your hands.'

'I want to go and see them right now,' she said. Her breath warmed his shirt. 'Sandie and

Chris, and their boys. I wish I could just get in the car and drive.'

'Can you do that?' He must have felt the tiny shake of her head against his shoulder. 'Why can't you?'

'They're an hour and forty minutes from here. It's a big property, called Comden Reach. I have to pick up Josh. It's not a good road at night. Dark, no traffic, and—'

'They're not very good reasons, Caroline.' His voice resonated in her ear, achingly close.

'OK. No. Declan, I can't…confront her with this, open my arms to her and start sobbing, if there's a chance she has no idea yet what this is about. It has to come from her doctor, who'll be able to answer her questions. And it has to be in a setting—her doctor's office—where she'll at least be a little prepared. I have to wait.'

'What if she does have an idea?'

'Then why on earth didn't she phone, or why didn't Chris? To talk to me?'

'So you're hurt, too, aren't you?'

'Which is so selfish! This isn't about me but, yes, if that's the case, if she suspected something was wrong, then I'm hurt. I could have helped. I hope. I care about both of them.

I would have wanted to try to help, anyway. I don't know what to feel.'

'And that can be the worst part of it sometimes. Clear-cut feelings are easier.'

His hand still washed up and down her back, like a chamois cloth polishing a cosseted car, careful and soft. Her forehead had glued itself to his shoulder, and her neck muscles refused to lift her head. He smelled good. He felt good—his warm arms, his strong legs. Most importantly, he kept saying the right things. But she couldn't stay in this position any longer. It just wasn't right.

'Thanks,' she said.

Her voice whispered harshly through her tightened throat, and her head came up at last—up far enough to bring his neck and jaw in line with her vision, just an inch or two away. Something jolted and coiled low inside her. Heavy. Strong as a train.

She stepped back to safety, frightened of the power of this full, physical yearning in her body. Her lips almost tingled with the desire to press herself against his skin. She felt heavy inside. She hadn't responded to a man this strongly—and this inappropriately—since she'd been in her teens. She ought to have more self-control. Declan's narrowed eyes raked over her tight face, and she could see him rethinking what he'd been about to say before he even said it.

'Listen, you said the road to their place wasn't safe at night.' He spoke slowly. 'For you and Josh alone, you mean? Because if you do want to go out there tonight, I could come with you and—'

'No.' She cut him off with a decisiveness that he surely wouldn't ignore. 'That's... unbelievably kind of you, but I think it would be wrong.'

'For you?'

'For Sandie and Chris. I know she might be on tenterhooks, but it's important that she hears a proper report, in the right way. The more I think about it, the more I'm convinced of that.'

He nodded, his eyes smoky and thoughtful and his mouth straight and closed.

'I'm not sure if she's even realised that I would see the slide,' Caroline went on, speaking too fast. 'I try not to think too much about patient names, because between us we all know a lot of people in this town, and it can be a burden, but how could I not think about

Sandie's? No, I'll—I'll wait. For her sake. I'll phone her in a day or two, when she'll definitely have heard.'

'And then you'll go out there?'

'Yes, on the weekend. Friday night, perhaps.'

'Drive safely, Caroline,' he said quietly. 'When you do go out there.'

The words stayed in her mind all the way home.

Declan had told Caroline to drive safely, but he'd come so close to offering, once again, to drive her to her brother and sister-in-law's farm himself. He knew he'd made the right decision in not doing so, although he didn't analyse the reasons too closely. He needed to focus on Suzy. He was no knight in shining armour, coming to the aid of a woman he barely knew. He and Caroline had a pleasant office friendship, one he'd begun to rely on and enjoy, but that was all.

At home, Suzy stared at her bright computer screen. The room had darkened around her and she hadn't got up from her desk to turn on the light.

'Are you interruptable?' he asked her.

'No.'

'Want some wine?'

'Yes. Something to eat? Crackers and cheese?'

'Coming up.'

'Sorry. Want to get this right before I stop.' Her fingers clattered on the keys, then flicked the mouse to highlight and delete a couple of lines.

The final draft of this episode was due on Friday, and he assumed that was when she'd head back to Sydney, to deliver it in person. She had a meeting scheduled, too, apparently. He'd asked her this morning how the script was coming along, and she'd said, 'Close.' In a writer's case, close was a stretchy word.

He brought her a glass of wine and a pile of crackers and cheese, and she grunted an acknowledgement and kept typing. He didn't resent it. She was a professional, and from what he'd read of her work, he had an idea that she was good.

Scripts were hard to read, though. They were full of choppy scene changes and directions as to interior or exterior, night or day. There was very little poetry in the language. It was probably as hard for him to assess her work with any accuracy as it would be for her to assess his.

He revised his wish-list for Suzy's future visits. Maybe she shouldn't come down when she had a looming deadline. Physically, they might be under the same roof, right now, but emotionally she was far away. He'd really been hoping for a nice night tonight. Hell, what would he have done if Caroline had taken him up on that half-reluctant offer to drive her and Josh out to her brother's right away?

Her emotions had been so complex and powerful that he'd forgotten about any other obligations at the time, and that troubled him. Damsels in distress could present unexpected dangers.

On the other hand, if Suzy stayed chained to her computer for much longer, a four-hour round trip into sheep country wouldn't have deprived him of her company any more than her work was already doing.

He prowled, turned on the television for some news, didn't know what to do with himself. 'Shall I cook?' he asked Suzy, interrupting again.

She half turned her head from the computer, kept her eyes on the screen. 'No, this is fine.' She still had crackers and cheese on the plate.

Fine for her, but he was hungry so, after waiting another half-hour or so, he knocked together an Asian-style noodle soup with some peanuts, green onions and a tin of baby shrimp, leaving a good percentage of it in case Suzy got hungry later after all.

She emerged finally at just before ten, frowning.

'I'll have to go back tomorrow,' she said. 'There's this scene at a marina I need to research. I've got the gun going into the— OK, no, I know, you don't need that level of detail.' She stretched her jaw, worked the tension out of her face with her fingers, then reached back and massaged a stiff spot in her spine. 'Let's go out somewhere and eat.'

'Now?' he answered blankly.

She grinned, her eyes sparkling. 'Why not?'

Because it's a Monday, and this is a country town, and even if we don't get dirty looks from the staff of the two restaurants that might conceivably still be open, the food'll probably be getting very tired. Unless we go for hamburgers and fries.

He didn't say it. For some reason, he couldn't be bothered.

'Feel like fast food?' he asked, instead.

'Lord, no! Out, Declan. Somewhere nice.'

'You have no idea what time it is, do you?'

She took it badly and wouldn't be comforted by the left-over noodle soup, now two hours old. His feelings about her returning to Sydney so soon took second place. In fact, they never got to those at all, and the evening limped along with both of them still prickly and distant and not finding any common ground.

'Come to Sydney yourself,' she suggested finally. 'Couldn't you? This weekend, or next? It's no fun when we can't go out.'

'This weekend I've said I'd play tennis again. Next weekend I'm on call. But the weekend after...'

'On call for looking down a microscope?'

He considered an explanation. Sure, as a pathologist he wasn't likely to get many emergency callouts, but if his pager did go off on a weekend, it went off for a good reason.

He took a breath, intending to sketch a couple of graphic examples for Suzy's benefit, but she had already turned away to rummage in the pantry.

'I just don't *feel* like Asian noodles from a packet, Dec. I'm starving! Bwah-ha-ha-ha!' She mimicked a spoiled, whining child. 'I want... I want... I want something fabulous and delicious and huge. A big plate of pasta from Bill and Toni's. Mushroom risotto. Vietnamese beef with lemon grass. Gourmet pizza. Followed by sticky date pudding or tiramisu.'

'You want to be in Sydney.'

She looked at him, head tilted, hands on hips. 'Well, don't you?'

'I don't spend a lot of energy on wanting things I can't have. That only makes you hungrier.'

She gave an exaggerated sigh, and a pout, and a smile with a dimple. 'OK, I'll cook eggs. Want some?'

'No, thanks. I just don't *feel* like eggs right now.'

She recognised that he was teasing her, burst out laughing and threw a teatowel at his head. The atmosphere eased again, and he remembered all the reasons he'd been prepared to follow her to Australia.

But something struck him, at eleven, as he rolled into bed—on his own, because Suzy had

had an idea and had gone back to her computer to key in some quick notes. When you had a relationship in which no statement of commitment had been made, he realised, you needed to feed it more constantly with time spent in each other's company.

You had to keep the reasons you were good together right there in front of you. You couldn't afford to be apart for too long, when the relationship was about *now* because, without *now* there was nothing left.

He got out of bed again and went to interrupt Suzy for the fourth or fifth time.

'If you go back to Sydney tomorrow,' he said, 'to research the gun and the marina, does that mean you'll have the draft in on Friday morning and can head down here for the weekend?'

'I'll try,' she answered, frowning at the screen.

Caroline made herself wait all through Tuesday without phoning Sandie and Chris.

Hiding it on the outside, she anguished within. Chris and his family saw a doctor who worked mainly in Glenfallon itself, but he had an office and surgery in the tiny town of

Cargoola, much closer to the farm, where he had appointments one day a week.

Which day?

She couldn't remember.

I'll phone Wednesday evening, she decided.

But Sandie got in first. Caroline picked up the phone on her desk at eleven on Wednesday morning and heard her sister-in-law's voice. She knew straight away that Sandie had been told about the results of the fine needle aspiration.

'I'm in town, Caroline,' she said, in a high, tight tone. 'C-could we have lunch? There's something I need to talk to you about.'

'Oh, Sandie, you've just seen Dr Malvern?'

'Yes, how did you—?'

'I looked at your slides. It's my job, Sandie.'

'Of course. I didn't even think. I somehow assumed they'd, I don't know, send it to Canberra. Or— I just wasn't thinking. So you know the whole story?'

'I know the diagnosis. But I'm not sure of everything your doctor will have told you. Look, do you want to come here? It's early, but we could go to the café…'

'I'll be there in five minutes.'

Caroline met Declan in the corridor on her way out. 'Eating early?' He smiled, looking very casual.

'I'm meeting Sandie. My sister-in-law.'

His face changed. 'Oh, lord, of course! I'm sorry.'

'No. No, it's fine.'

'So she's heard?'

'Yes. At least it's in the open now, and I can talk to her about it. She sounds upset.'

'She'll be too upset to think straight today,' he predicted. 'It's later the flood of questions will come.'

'Josh and I will go out to the farm on Saturday, first thing. He can miss soccer.'

Declan leaned against the corridor wall, absently rubbing his palm over the semi-gloss paintwork at shoulder height. 'Listen, can I repeat my offer to drive you out? I wouldn't let you behind the wheel of a car, the way you look at the moment.'

'By Saturday—'

'By Saturday you won't care any more, is that it?'

He drew a reluctant, upside down laugh from her. 'Oh, you're right, but I can't let you go to—'

'You can please, pretty please with bells on, "let" me, Caroline. Suzy's not coming down, she told me last night. I'll be bored. I'd like to see some of the country while I'm here. Some of those sheep's backs you lot supposedly ride on.'

She couldn't have accepted the offer as a favour to herself, but now that he'd twisted it around to make it a favour to him, she couldn't refuse.

And didn't want to. She knew quite well the reason, and recognised a whole strand of feeling inside herself that existed quite separately from her anguish over Sandie.

How much of a sin was it to like a man this much when he was already committed elsewhere?

Not much, surely. She had no dark intentions. She'd turn this into a friendship with him, if she could. With Suzy, too, if she ever spent any time here. And she'd suffer the deeper attraction in silence until it went away, while keeping a scrupulous façade in place so that Declan didn't suspect.

These sorts of things did go away eventually, didn't they?

They had to.

'It would be great to have another adult,' she said slowly. 'And you'll be able to answer more of Sandie's questions than I can. But I'll have to ask her how she feels about it.'

'Of course. Just let me know.'

Caroline didn't spend long with her sister-in-law over lunch. Sandie was due to meet Chris at the hardware store soon.

'I didn't have a clue,' she said. She looked pale and wrung out, with her light brown hair dragged back into a low, bushy ponytail at the back that didn't suit her. Her casual pink top and dark trousers hung on her, showing the weight she'd lost. She moved as if any exertion was an effort.

'I wasn't even worried,' she continued. 'I really thought Dr Malvern would just tell me I was stressed and exhausted and I should eat better and slow down. He didn't say anything about why he wanted the various tests. I was all prepared to tell him what an impossible piece of medical advice ''slowing down'' would be for me, with the boys and the farm.'

'So Chris doesn't know yet?'

'No.'

'What do you need to know, Sandie? What more did Dr Malvern tell you?'

'There's only one thing I need to know,' she said, her voice smoky with unshed tears. 'That I'm going to live.'

'Of course you're going to live! You're going to be fine. We're not going to consider anything else.'

CHAPTER SIX

DECLAN picked up Caroline and Josh from their house at nine on Saturday morning, after he'd phoned her the previous evening to check that Sandie was happy to have a stranger at Comden Reach. Apparently she was. That was nice of her.

He probably should have reneged on Sunday tennis after Suzy had phoned on Tuesday night to tell him—big surprise!—that she wasn't coming down. Tom and the others would have understood if he'd said he was going to Sydney instead. But he was angry, dissatisfied. If he went to Sydney this weekend, he knew he'd feel as if Suzy was calling all the shots. They'd have a bad time.

So he'd stayed here in Glenfallon out of pride and…something else. Caution. Cold feet. He didn't know what name to give the way he felt. He did know he felt restless, ready to do more than mow the lawn, rent a video and stock up on groceries.

The weather was gorgeous. He'd have considered it worthy of high summer in Ireland, or even in London. Here it was just another mild, cloudless autumn day. In the back seat of his car, Caroline's dark-haired, freckle-nosed eleven-year-old sat quietly. The motion sickness tablet always made him drowsy, Caroline said. From the little Declan had seen of Josh, he seemed like a nice kid. Big smile, crooked teeth and a little goofy and vague, as Declan had been himself at that age.

Caroline was pretty quiet as well, during a drive that took more than an hour and a half, but she was a long way from going to sleep. Every time he glanced sideways, he saw the tense angles of her limbs and the frown on her face. The farther they got from Glenfallon, the better he understood.

The irrigated stretches of lush green citrus fruit and trellised vines only reached a couple of kilometres beyond the river. After that, they crossed a range of low hills and saw the vast expanse of the western plains. They were flatter than the ocean and still terribly dry. There had been some rain in February, apparently. It had helped. Declan saw streaks of green. But it hadn't been enough.

Untidy flocks of sheep, their coats the colour of brown dust, eked out enough sustenance in their huge paddocks somehow. Hard to imagine that before the recent rains, the country had looked even worse. His Irish eyes couldn't find this landscape beautiful, but he understood its power and its pull. Beauty wasn't everything. Something stirred in him that he'd never felt in London or Sydney—a sense of awe, and an emotional response to the land itself.

The distances were so vast out here, and the work was so hard. Caroline's brother and his family must already be stretched thin. How on earth would the McLennans accommodate Sandie's vital cancer treatment into their lives, for the next six months and possibly more? Caroline would have to find a way to help. He didn't doubt that she'd do it.

'How old are the boys?' he asked.

'Chris and Sandie's boys? Seven and four.'

Caroline looked good today, despite her inner turmoil. She wore snug-fitting jeans, white running shoes and a light, Wedgwood blue cotton sweater that showed off her shapely figure subtly. She had her glossy hair up in a high ponytail that made her look at least five years younger than she really was. He was more aware of her seated beside him than he wanted to be.

'How will they manage?' He threw her another quick glance, drawn by the complex expressions that crossed her face.

'I'm going to offer to have the boys stay with me while Sandie is having the treatment in Canberra,' she said, 'as well as during the recovery phase following each cycle. And I'm sure Chris will take me up on it. He can't run the farm and look after the boys on his own.'

'Can you handle that?'

'I'll have to.'

He couldn't help contrasting her matter-of-fact determination with Suzy's various blithe, beguiling promises over the past few months, which wasn't fair.

It wasn't fair, so he dropped it, refused to think about it. He'd go to Sydney in two weeks and put his cards on the table. He'd given a lot to the relationship already, by moving ten thousand miles. He'd give more—he'd consider marriage—if Suzy would meet him halfway. Having settled that, it would be best if he didn't think about Suzy at all.

'Mattie's at school, so he's less of a concern,' Caroline said.

'Not in Glenfallon?' He dragged his thoughts back to someone else's problems. 'That'd be a hell of a bus ride.'

'No, in Cargoola. We'll be driving through it soon. It's tiny. They have a two-room school. You'll laugh at it, after London. Mattie can switch to Josh's school for a couple of terms. Josh will look after him, and he'll fit right back in at Cargoola later.'

'Sounds like it, if it's that small.'

'Sam would be at preschool, only there's no preschool in Cargoola. I'll have to put him into child-care. And I've asked Natalia if she'll increase her hours, so I can cut down on mine.'

Declan forced down an instant disappointment at the thought of not having Caroline around for half of every working day. He liked Tom and Steph and the others, but had already concluded that Caroline was the only one he could really talk to. Better than he and Suzy talked, in some ways.

Dangerous ground, Declan.

He knew it, and felt rebellious once more, angry with Suzy and with himself. 'Because it's fun' wasn't a good enough reason for two people to be together.

'She thinks that'll be fine,' Caroline went on, 'but she wants to make sure Alexei agrees.'

'You've really thought about it.'

Again, he had to remind himself that comparisons weren't fair. 'Come to Sydney with me,' Suzy had said. How much thinking had she done before she'd issued that saucy, I-dare-you invitation?

'I don't want Sandie coming up with objections I haven't got an answer for,' Caroline said. 'In situations like this, people tend to say a vague, open ended sort of, "If there's anything you need..." and that doesn't really help. It has to be a concrete offer, with all the objections already ironed out.' He saw her blink back tears. 'If I'd spent more time out here over the past month or two, I might have seen that something was wrong. I won't let Chris and Sandie down again.'

Declan wanted to tell her not to be so hard on herself, that she put herself down too often, but he held it back. He was starting to feel as if he was wearing an emotional strait-jacket today.

They drove through Cargoola and, yes, he could easily have laughed at how small the brightly painted school buildings were. Ten kilometres beyond the town, a line of trees loomed larger, getting closer and closer on their left. The big eucalyptuses marked the river, whose course would converge with theirs as they reached the McLennans' farm. The place was much prettier than Declan had expected, an oasis of quiet, lush beauty in this uncompromising landscape.

The homestead and outbuildings were set just beyond the slope that would mark the furthest reach of the river in all but the most severe floods. Chris and Sandie had worked incredibly hard here, and obviously took pride in what they'd achieved. Climbing from the car, he took in as much as he could.

The buildings were all painted cream, with dark red roofs that contrasted with the green of the surprisingly lush gardens around them. Wide verandas on three sides of the house were set with cane furniture, potted palms and children's toys.

Declan recognised Australian native shrubs and South African proteas, some of them in flower, a small orchard, vegetables and herbs, some huge pine trees that must have been here for a century, and two sloping beds of fussy, thirsty European plants such as roses and petunias just below the front veranda.

A row of large rainwater tanks, fed by run-off from the roof, explained how they'd managed to keep the garden going without significant rain for so long. He also saw something that might be a pump-house, bringing water up from the river.

Before he could take in anything more, a side door opened and a thin, fair woman who must be Sandie McLennan came towards them, with her boys frisking ahead of her, along with a pair of black and white sheep-dogs. In a state of high excitement, boys and dogs immediately latched onto big cousin Josh, who quickly shook off his drowsiness and allowed himself to be taken off to see some boy thing of enormous and urgent importance. Focused on Sandie, Caroline broke into a fast stride that was almost a run, and hugged her, tears streaming down her cheeks.

'We hardly talked the other day,' she said. 'It's so good to be here. I'm sorry. We haven't been since January...'

'Well, it's been so hot till recently. You've had school, work... And we've seen you in town.'

'That's no excuse, Sandie.'

Caroline's brother appeared, and she hugged him, too, then took his face between her hands and searched it for the signs of strain she must have known she'd find there. 'Ugly mug,' she said. 'The beard's good. Covers you up a bit.'

Declan stifled a smile, feeling a little out of place. The boys and the dogs had disappeared completely. He could hear barks and shouts coming from behind a couple of sheds. Caroline had forgotten to introduce him. She'd forgotten he was there, in fact. Remembering, she looked remorseful.

'Oh, I'm sorry! Chris, Sandie, this is our new—'

'Chauffeur,' Declan said, stepping forward. 'And tourist.'

'Pathologist. And godsend,' Caroline corrected. 'Only he's temporary.' She smiled her warm, lovely smile. 'That's the only thing we don't like about him.'

Chris came up and gave him a hearty handshake—the kind of handshake a protective brother gives when he's wondering if this is his divorced little sister's new boyfriend.

'My…uh…partner—girlfriend—is in Sydney,' Declan explained. 'I can't get a position there until I've sat some exams.'

I shouldn't have come, he realised as Chris nodded and said, 'Right. I see.'

It's the wrong time, the wrong circumstances and I'm the wrong person.

Too late to reach that conclusion. He'd hold back as much as he could, try not to get in the way. Maybe he'd play with the boys, keep them out of the way, too, so that Chris and Sandie and Caroline could talk about plans.

'Declan seems nice,' Sandie offered, as she and Caroline washed the dishes together, following a barbecue lunch that they'd somehow managed to keep relaxed and pleasant.

'He's great. We wish we could keep him. Tom is torturing himself with an unrealistic hope that it's possible.'

'Why isn't it?'

'The girlfriend. She's very Sydney. So's he, really. He was living in London before. Not a country person.'

'Hmm.'

'What's that for?'

'You don't like the girlfriend, do you?'

'Nope. Totally unfair of me, I've only met her once. I should have met her more! She was supposed to come down, but she hardly has, and I can tell he's disappointed.'

'Hmm,' said Sandie again.

There was a silence, and Caroline knew exactly what she was thinking. Her resistance crumbled at once. 'OK, I admit it,' she said.

'Yeah, I thought so.' They'd known each other for more than ten years.

'Is it obvious?'

'Only to me, I should think.'

'I'm trying to hide it. I thought I was. I hate it.'

'Chris wondered at first, but once Declan mentioned the girlfriend, any suspicion was lulled. It wouldn't occur to him that you could feel something if the man was attached.'

'He's right. I shouldn't.'

'But you can't help what you feel, of course you can't, and I know you wouldn't act on it. Your brother is so...' Sandie sniffed, and sobbed and laughed at herself '...faithful.' She broke down completely, and had to reach for the tissues on top of the fridge. 'I'm so lucky, Caroline! I love him so much, and the boys. If this treatment doesn't work... I just can't bear the thought. And I haven't got *time* for the treatment!'

'Listen, this is what I've worked out.' Caroline's throat ached, but she forced herself to speak steadily. 'Don't worry about time. You'll be able to give everything you need to, to the treatment and to getting well, eating right, getting enough rest, because that's what we all want.'

They talked for half an hour, finished the dishes, made a cup of tea and got it all sorted out. The boys would come to Caroline during the week for the next two school terms and longer if necessary, with weekends split between Glenfallon and the farm. Sandie could get her six week-long cycles of treatment and her three weeks of rest after each one, and Chris would handle the farm.

'I don't want to be parted from any of them for even a day,' Sandie said, 'but I know that's not realistic. They'll have a great time with you.'

While they talked, Caroline assumed that Chris was entertaining Declan, and that the boys were entertaining themselves, but then Chris wandered in and announced that he'd got the tractor fixed, and she asked him blankly, 'With Declan?'

'No, he's with the boys.'

'I thought you were showing him the river.'

'Well, I was going to, but then he said could the boys do that, and they were keen so I let them and got on with a couple of jobs. Seems nice. A bit...not standoffish, but...'

'Reserved,' Sandie suggested, shooting a quick glance at Caroline, who bit her lip.

Declan's keeping out of our way, she realised. He thinks he has to.

She heard voices and thumping footsteps at that moment, and the three boys arrived in the kitchen in a noisy heap, with Declan just behind them. The dogs were left by the steps—callously abandoned, their barking whines insisted. They begged unsuccessfully to be let inside.

'Declan doesn't know *anything*, Mum,' Mattie announced. 'He asked if we rode the sheep.'

'He said they looked lovely and comfortable!' Sam giggled.

'He said did we have a pig for a sheep-dog like in *Babe*.'

'He said did the sheep have saddles!'

'He was just kidding, you know,' Josh came in, but he was grinning.

'He's hilarious!'

'You're a hit, Dr McCulloch,' Sandie said. She touched Declan on the arm and handed him a cup of tea, as if he were family. Caroline's heart lurched.

Almost two weeks passed.

Sandie went to Canberra with Chris for her first debilitating cycle of treatment and returned, exhausted and nauseous, to the farm. Meanwhile, the boys came to Glenfallon and seemed to slot into their new lives with reassuring ease. The two-week Easter school break ended.

Mattie and Sam knew their mother was sick, but they didn't know how sick, and they believed, one hundred per cent, that the treatment would make her better. It would have been cruel and pointless, at this stage, to shatter their beautiful, heart-nourishing faith by telling them that there was any other possibility.

At the end of Mattie's and Sam's first week of school and child-care in Glenfallon, Caroline and Josh had to go to Sydney for the open day at Woodside. With her working hours now limited to mornings, she could pick Mattie up from school early and drive him and Sam out to the farm to spend the weekend, and still get back in time for a four o'clock start to Sydney.

All the same, the three-hour round trip—three and a half, really, once Caroline had unloaded the boys' overnight bags and talked to Chris and Sandie for a few minutes—added considerably to the driving time she'd have to put in today. It couldn't be helped. She'd handle it.

What she couldn't handle, and what nearly had her in tears, was the sudden death of her engine five kilometres out of town on the return journey. She smelled the hot odour of oil, and knew something was seriously wrong.

A passing traveller responded to her signal and stopped to help. He had a mobile phone, so she could call the motorists' association road service. The mechanic showed up within half an hour, and told her she had no oil left. The car was on its second trip around the mileage clock and must have developed a slow leak. The engine had seized. Possibly she'd cracked the engine block. She'd have to get towed to the garage in Glenfallon for investigation and repair, and there was no question of getting to Sydney today in this vehicle.

'But I have to get to Sydney!' she told the mechanic.

He shrugged, and gave an upside down smile. 'You could stick out your thumb, hitch a ride.'

She nodded. 'I will. I'll have to. Not literally, but I do know someone else who's driving up today.'

She phoned Declan at the pathology department within ten minutes of getting home, relieved to find he hadn't yet left. Josh had his overnight bag packed and waiting in the hall, and was eating a banana in front of the television. It was already after four-thirty.

'And I'm only asking because I'm really desperate, Declan. The two flights are full. The bus has already gone through, and the train would have, too, by the time I could organise someone to drive us the fifty kilometres to—'

'Shush, look, it's no problem.'

'But I feel I'm...'

Tricking you into this.

Doing it because I want to spend time in your company.

And being way too obvious about it.

None of that was true, but it was how she felt.

She gave Josh his motion sickness pill and threw her own gear together, which she hadn't had a chance to do before, and they waited for Declan on the front porch because she didn't want to delay him for a second longer than necessary.

He was very good about it. Polite and cheerful and relaxed, dressed casually in jeans that made her aware, as always, of his capable, masculine body. If this was a nuisance, he didn't let it show, even when he discovered that the motel where she and Josh were staying was in Pymble. It was close to Woodside and Robert's and Gail's house, but well north of the Harbour Bridge. Declan himself was headed for Coogee, almost as far from the bridge in the opposite direction.

For the first two hours or more, Caroline pretended to be asleep, as Josh was, then she felt the car slowing, opened her eyes and saw that Declan was pulling into a fast-food place just off the highway. They ate spicy chicken burgers and fries, washed down with soft drinks.

'Lord, but junk food can taste good in the middle of a long drive!' Declan said. 'I'm not sure if it's the fat, the additives or the salt.'

Josh grinned at the statement, and took a big bite of his own burger, nodding his head in fervent agreement. With Josh so sleepy until now, the two of them hadn't spoken very much, but they seemed relaxed with each other.

Caroline had noticed this two weeks ago on the farm, too. Declan seemed to have very clear memories of what being a pre-teen boy meant, and males didn't always need a lot of conversation to establish common ground.

'Would you like me to drive for a while, Declan?' she offered.

'If you don't mind. Between the microscope, the computer and the car, my shoulders are ready for a break.'

Again, nobody talked much. Caroline could see that Declan was tired, although he insisted on taking the wheel again after she'd driven for two hours. They didn't get to Pymble until nearly midnight, which meant it would be close to one in the morning by the time Declan crossed back through the Harbour tunnel and through the eastern suburbs to Coogee.

'What time shall I pick you up on Sunday?' he asked her.

'Oh, don't,' she told him. 'I mean, we'll make our way to you, if you'll give me the address and tell me what time you want to start.'

'Three? Is that too late?'

'Whenever you want.'

'We'll eat on the road again.'

'That's fine.' She took down the address and phone number quickly, and didn't delay him any further.

The next day, touring Josh's potential future school with his father, she had to agree that Woodside was beautiful, and luxuriously endowed with every facility and every extra-curricular programme an ambitious parent could want.

Josh quickly disappeared with a crowd of other boys his age to submit to the tests that would determine whether he met the necessary threshold of academic excellence. In that area, Caroline wasn't concerned. He wasn't a brilliant student, but he was bright enough. As soon as he'd gone, she took a deep breath and prepared to cover the same territory she and Robert had already been through.

He couldn't be swayed, however. He hadn't asked for much over the past ten years in the area of their son's upbringing, he pointed out, and it was true. He'd never failed to pay child support, never reneged on a holiday visit. This one thing he wanted for his son. It would help them to build a better bond.

'He's not going to enjoy boarding, and being so far away,' Caroline argued. 'He's not someone who likes big groups of kids and organised activities every minute. He likes time to himself. He's behaved so responsibly since he's started coming home from school on his own. Jenny Hollis, next door, is so impressed.'

And he's all I've got.

She was wise enough not to let this particular argument slip out. She'd have sacrificed her own feelings if she'd sincerely thought boarding at Woodside would be good for Josh.

'That's not the point,' Robert said. 'It's the opportunities he'll get, the time we'll have, the contacts he'll make.'

'I don't want him to have contacts. I want him to have friends. Ranleigh is—'

'Please, let's not talk any more about Ranleigh, Caroline. It's not in the same class as Woodside, even if a comparison of schools was the only issue. As I've said, I haven't asked for much. This is important to me.'

She fell back to a more conciliatory position that still had her stomach tying itself in knots, in anticipated loss. 'Then couldn't he live with you and Gail? I know he'd like that better.'

Robert didn't answer for some seconds. Caroline watched him, trying to read his face. He'd put on weight in recent years, and had begun to look a little jowly. He parted his hair further to the side now, in an attempt to hide the fact that it was thinning. She was surprised Gail let him get away with it. Didn't all women prefer frank balding to an obvious comb-over of inadequate strands?

'Well, yes, I've considered that, but I don't think it would be appropriate, Caroline,' he said finally.

'Not *appropriate*? What do you mean?'

'I think it would be…difficult. With Amelia. There's too much potential for problems. You hear about cases of abuse by older siblings in blended families. It could be disastrous. At minimum, it would be unfair on her. And on Gail.'

Too shocked and angry to speak, Caroline felt her blood pressure build and her scalp muscles tighten. Yes, there'd be extra work for Gail, but this was Gail's husband's child. No one said a second marriage was an effortless bed of roses when there were children from the previous marriage involved. And was Robert seriously suggesting that his precious young daughter wouldn't be *safe* with an older half-brother around? Not safe with Josh, sweet-natured *Josh*, Robert's own son?

She couldn't believe it, and she wanted to yell. More rationally, she thought about sketching out to him how well Josh had handled Mattie and Sam, who were darlings but who could both be less than angelic at times, and had already broken a couple of Josh's old toys. She wanted to say how great it would be for the half-siblings to actually get to know each other and build a relationship. Robert himself had claimed that building relationships was important, after all.

Oh, hell! There was no point! She looked across at her ex-husband, and saw a gap she'd never be able to bridge. If he could speak as if he considered his own son capable of bullying a baby sister, or worse, then there was no point attempting to communicate on the issue.

How strongly did she feel about this question of boarding at Woodside? Would she risk taking the matter to family court?

Oh, it was miserable!

She almost hoped Josh would do badly in the tests and not earn a place there.

After the morning of tests came an afternoon of activities. An art exhibition, food stalls, sporting displays. Robert insisted on seeing all of it, and since they were going straight on to dinner with him and Gail and Amelia at their home, Caroline couldn't make an excuse to leave. If Robert thought he'd get Josh on side with all this action, then he didn't understand the problem.

'What do you think?' she whispered to her son, shortly before they left, at last.

'I like the pool,' he answered gloomily.

She guessed he'd never be able to articulate his reluctance very well, but that didn't mean it wasn't real, and worth taking seriously.

That evening, they all tried very hard. Gail asked lots of questions about Caroline's work, her house, her family, and Caroline reciprocated. She found Gail much easier to talk to than Robert now. Josh was gorgeous with Amelia, giving her 'horsy rides' on his back and making her shriek with laughter, but if Robert was in any way influenced by this, or if he even noticed, he didn't make any comment.

The next day, he and Gail had another commitment in the morning, thank goodness, so Caroline and Josh swam in the motel's heated pool and had a walk and bought some snacks to eat in the car on the way home. Robert had agreed to drive them to Coogee in the afternoon.

They arrived early, at a quarter to three, and Caroline didn't want to keep her ex-husband waiting around—or Declan, if he was ready to start ahead of time—so she went up the stairs to the top-floor unit and knocked straight away.

Suzy opened the door. Frowned. 'Oh, hi.'

'We're early. I hope—'

But Suzy had already disappeared, not interested in what Caroline hoped. It wasn't clear from her manner that she remembered who Caroline was, although surely she must.

Caroline stood and waited, staring at the white expanse of a door pushed back towards the jamb so that it was only just ajar. Declan appeared a few minutes later.

'The car's parked round the corner,' he said. He looked preoccupied. 'Let me help you transfer your gear. Do you want to come in for a minute?'

'No, I'm fine, thanks. Robert is waiting in the street with Josh.'

Beside Robert's car, she introduced the two men briefly, and asked Josh to help Declan with the overnight bags.

'So...' Robert said, as soon as Declan and Josh headed around the corner.

'Well, it's been interesting,' she answered brightly.

His face clouded. 'Better than that, I hope. Don't treat him like a baby, Caroline. That's the problem with being the single mother of a son. He's not getting enough male influence. It you want the truth, that's a big factor in my feeling so strongly about Woodside. Obviously the father-son relationship is the preferable one, but if there was some other decent man around for him, I'd be almost as happy. This guy Declan who drove you down...'

He tilted his head in the direction of Declan, who was just about to disappear around the corner into a side street. Parking was tight in this area, so near the beach, and Robert had been lucky to squeeze into a space in front of the building.

'Declan? Yes?'

'Do you have something going on? Are you involved?'

'No. He's—'

'You see, that would be the best argument against sending him to Woodside. If you were planning to marry again, to a successful, decent man. Josh would have the male influence then.'

'Right.'

It didn't make sense to Caroline. Josh already had his Uncle Chris on the farm, a male soccer coach, her father, until the recent experimental move to Queensland, and Robert himself during holiday visits. Tons of male influence. Again, she didn't argue the issue, and wondered, half flippant and half painfully serious, whether she should actively look for a new relationship.

She'd lost weight, felt more attractive than she had for several years, if not as confident as she'd have liked. And she'd seen her friends Kit and Emma find love with good men.

So, yes. Sure. She'd start answering personal ads, join a singles club or some organisation in which males predominated—the local volunteer bushfire service, perhaps. She'd circle the choppy waters of Glenfallon's dating scene like a shark, in search of a male influence for Josh. It didn't matter how much she actually liked the man herself.

Declan and Josh came back round the corner again towards Robert's car and the entrance to the block of units. Declan had his car keys jingling in his hand. He tossed them casually in the air and caught them again. Sunlight glinted on the metal of the keys, and brightened one side of his face. His eyes looked as blue as the sea that stretched to the horizon from the beach just beyond the far end of the street.

One look at him, and Caroline knew she wouldn't be answering any personal ads. Not yet. Not until she could get over this attraction that had hit her so unexpectedly over the past six weeks, and which had no possibility of a future.

'Well, we'll talk again soon,' Robert told her.

'Thanks for looking after us so well,' she answered.

They didn't touch. Hadn't for years.

He gave Josh the playful punch on the arm that he'd considered an appropriate degree of physical affection for his son since Josh was two, then climbed into his car and roared off up the street, back to the baby daughter he cuddled and talked baby talk to and bought presents for almost every week.

'I'll just say goodbye to Suzy,' Declan said, and loped up the stairs.

He wasn't gone for long.

They left on time, at three, and Josh was soon asleep in the back. He'd had a restless night, and the motion sickness tablet was having its usual effect.

'Did you have a good weekend, then?' Declan asked casually, after he'd turned into Alison Road.

'Oh, yes,' she answered. 'Woodside is fabulous. You start to understand why it's so expensive. Josh felt he did well in the tests. Robert thinks the school will be very good for him. And it was lovely to watch him and Amelia, his half-sister, together.'

Declan didn't say anything for a moment, then he glanced across at her and drawled, 'The last sentence I'll believe.'

'Oh. Only the last sentence?'

'Hey, didn't we more or less agree a month or so ago that we were going to be friends, and honest with each other?'

'We agreed that we were going to share a laugh sometimes, I thought.'

'Well, you can't share a laugh, if you're not being honest.'

'Maybe not,' she agreed cautiously.

Out of a short silence, she suddenly heard him swear under his breath, and glanced in his direction, automatically wondering, after her own experience on Friday, if there was something wrong with the car.

'Problem?' she asked.

He shook his head, frowning, a little distant in his thoughts. 'No,' he said. 'I've just... realised something, that's all.'

'Forgot your pillow?'

He laughed, then drawled, 'Nothing that dire.'

'Now it's you who's not being honest,' she said.

Silence.

'Thinking about my weekend,' he finally answered.

'Was it as good as mine?' She let the sarcasm show lightly in her tone.

So did he. 'Better, if that's possible,' he said. He hesitated. 'I...uh...yes.' He stopped again. 'Suzy's coming down next weekend.'

Which didn't tell Caroline very much.

He didn't seem inclined to go into any detail about the ambivalent mood she could sense in him, so she let it drop.

She found it much more difficult to go on hiding her own preoccupation. When you found someone easy to talk to, it was hard not to let everything spill out. 'I just don't want my son to go away to school,' she heard herself say...and didn't even have the excuse that alcohol had loosened her tongue today.

Maybe the smooth, hypnotic movement of the car along the multi-lane highway could have just as dangerous an effect. 'I think Robert is trying to remake Josh in his own image, and in his way he means well, but they're too different for that.'

'Is Josh more like you, then?'

'In some ways. And he's a lot like my father. Mostly, he's just himself.'

'Which is the best thing to be.'

'Absolutely. We—we didn't plan him. I was on the Pill. I was six hours late in taking it one crucial day, and that was all my system needed.'

'You must be very fertile.'

'I must have been. Then. I was only twenty-one. Robert took ages to accept that we were having a baby, but I was thrilled straight away. Robert will see more of Josh than I do if he goes to Woodside, and even though he talks about building a better relationship, and means it, I'm not convinced he'd notice if Josh was seriously unhappy, or going off the rails. He's very absorbed in Gail and Amelia, of course. It's right that he should be. But he makes the wrong assumptions about Josh.'

'I think a lot of parents do, particularly about their first-born, and especially when that first-born is of the same sex. My older sister got a heck of a hard time from my mother, growing up.'

'I haven't asked, Declan, are you from a large family?'

'Six.'

'Six!'

'What we lacked in material wealth, we made up for in companionship. And fights. We were like puppies, tumbling around the house.'

'And where did you fit in?'

'Third. You learn a lot about compromise. And a lot about grabbing what's on offer, whether you want it or not, before it disappears.'

'This was in Dublin? Belfast?'

'County Kerry, in a little town called Ballycarreal, in a little house next to the post office, with a garage just like your dad's. 'Twasn't the kind of Irish poverty that people write haunting novels about, but it had its memorable moments.'

The slight veneer of London that usually smoothed some of the curls off his accent peeled away as he talked about his childhood. Caroline listened, entranced by what he said, entranced by his voice and his tone and the expressions that crossed his face, and very glad they were talking about him, not her. She didn't want to go whining on and on about Josh and Robert.

'You must miss the green of the fields,' she said.

'But not the rain that makes them that way.'

'Rain! If you could arrange to get some sent across, we'd love it.'

He laughed, then asked, 'How are the little boys settling in, by the way?'

'Oh, they're sweet. And a handful. It was the right thing to do. Chris is bringing them into town first thing in the morning. I know Sandie just won't get enough rest with them around for more than a day or two at a stretch. It's hard for her. She's missed them terribly for the past ten days, even though they've talked on the phone every night.'

'Do the boys know much about what's going on?'

'Not much.' She told him about their utter faith in their mum getting well, and confessed, 'Sometimes, sharing their faith is the only thing that keeps the rest of us going, I think.'

'Who're the rest of you? I mean, besides the obvious. You and Chris and Sandie herself.'

'Well, there's her two sisters, near Wentworth and Holbrook, and Chris's and my parents, whose house you're renting. They're coming down soon, by the way, for a visit. I get the impression they're not enjoying the Gold Coast lifestyle as much as they expected to. Sandie's illness has given them a shock, too.'

'Family pulls more strongly at such times.'

'Where are your brothers and sisters, Declan?'

'Scattered all over the world, which means I feel the family pull in about six different directions and have to make my own way. London seemed the obvious choice.'

'You trained there?'

'Yes, and stayed on afterwards. Meanwhile, my parents are still in the same house we grew up in. They've no plans to move.'

'And I wouldn't be surprised if Mum and Dad end up back in Glenfallon.'

'I like Glenfallon,' Declan said. 'A lot more than I expected to.'

As much as Sydney? More than London?

Caroline caught herself just in time, and managed not to make a Tom-like, over-enthusiastic response to his statement.

'A few people seem to find that,' she said instead, in a much more neutral tone. 'Their prejudices against Australian country towns fade once they settle in.'

'Yes, as a year's exile, it could be a lot worse.'

She gave a stricken cry. 'Exile!' Then she saw how he was laughing at her, and laughed, too. 'You're good, Dr McCulloch!'

They went on talking, and Caroline was astonished when she saw the fast food and petrol signs at the far end of the Yass bypass, just ahead. Had they come this far? It hadn't felt nearly that long. She'd been too content, and too interested in their conversation, to notice.

CHAPTER SEVEN

THE woman going into the supermarket looked vaguely familiar, Declan realised at once. She smiled at him in a tentative way, not quite meeting his eye. With Suzy pushing the trolley of filled grocery bags ahead of him, he stopped and racked his brains, trying to put the woman in context.

Someone from the hospital. Around forty years old, with dark blonde hair, freckly skin and a reserved way of holding her body that hinted at a strong need for distance and privacy. Someone who—

Click.

'Hi!' he said, feeling his interest rise. 'Hello!'

This was the patient whose sister had yelled at her, five or six weeks ago, because she'd left a breast lump unexamined and untreated for so long that it had become an open wound. He remembered the emotion they'd all felt, and had to suppress a shiver of reaction.

'Hello, Dr McCulloch.' She smiled again.

'You're back in Glenfallon. I'm sorry, I know exactly who you are, but I've forgotten your name.'

'Alison. Alison Scanlon.'

'That's right. You're back from Canberra.'

'Just for the weekend. I still have another week of treatment.' The corners of her mouth turned down in a wry expression. 'But I needed a break, and it's my sister's birthday, so I came back.'

'You're looking good.'

'Feeling a bit better,' she agreed cautiously.

Declan was immediately pleased that he'd run into her. He glanced through the automatic doors and saw Suzy waiting beyond them. She looked back at him, frowning and impatient. Well, she could wait a couple of minutes, couldn't she?

'The oncologist is pleased with how the tumour is responding,' Alison said. 'But they did a scan and there's something on my ovary as well.'

The tone suggested she was reporting a wart on her knee, but she would have been told what the 'something' on her ovary meant. Metastasis. A spread of the cancer beyond the primary tumour in her breast to other parts of her body. In no way was it anything other than disastrous news.

Declan could only nod.

'OK,' he added, to make his response just marginally less inadequate.

'I'm booked in, here in Glenfallon, for the ovary and the, um, other place, as soon as the treatment's finished in Canberra,' she told him, and he knew that he or Tom would therefore be the first to learn her prognosis.

It would probably be him, Declan realised. Tom was mainly tackling other areas of pathology, such as blood analysis and biochemistry, and leaving the anatomical pathology to him now that he was on board.

In around ten days, Declan would examine some cell clusters and some fragments of tissue, with this woman's whole life hanging on what he saw. And the prognosis would almost certainly be dire. He didn't look forward to making it, and he knew Alison's GP would hate having to give her the news, no matter what stage of acceptance she might have reached.

Suzy abandoned the trolley and strode back through the automatic doors. 'Are you coming,

Declan? Or…?' She tossed a cool, uninterested glance at Alison.

'Good luck,' Declan said to the woman. 'Are you here on your own?'

'My sister dropped me off. She's parking. We're getting a ton of fruit and vegetables. She's nagging me to death about eating right. Everyone is.'

She grinned suddenly, still managing to look shy and reserved even when the smile lit up her whole face. And Declan knew that at least she'd been given this gift of truly understanding how much she meant to her family.

'Well, as I said, all the luck in the world, Alison.'

'Who was that?' Suzy asked outside a few minutes later.

'A patient.' He took over the trolley.

'I thought you saw cells and tissue, not patients.'

'Sometimes I see actual patients. More than I used to in London. She's one of them.'

'Interesting?'

'Yes.'

But he didn't want to talk about it. Suzy got angry, in a teasing sort of way. 'Hey, doesn't it ever occur to you, McCulloch, that I might be able to *use* some of this stuff?'

'That's what I'm afraid of.'

'Oh, honestly, Dec, I'd change the details, of course. Actually, I need an illness right now, in Episode Six, where the character has to be at death's door, and then—'

'Not this illness. Not today. Let's talk about where we're going for our picnic.'

'Yeah, the picnic, that's going to be fun.'

'Is that the best you ever look for in anything, Suzy?' Declan heard himself say. 'That it's going to be fun?'

He saw her startled, uncomprehending, let's-not-spoil-the-moment expression, and knew that they had to talk.

This weekend.

Caroline had a cup of tea in her hand, on the way back to her office, when she heard Declan's phone ring in the office just along the corridor. Declan heard it, too, and looked up from the multi-header microscope, where he was giving Natalia his opinion on a difficult slide. He saw Caroline in the doorway.

'Want me to get it?' she offered.

'Yes, if you could.'

She put the tea down on her desk, crossed to his office and grabbed the phone. 'Declan McCulloch's line.'

'Caroline?' She heard her friend Nell Cassidy's voice.

'Yes, hi, Nell. He's on the multi-header. Can I take a message?'

'Could I speak to him? He'll want to hear this. You will, too, come to think of it. I've just assisted with the biopsy on Alison Scanlon's breast and the removal of the ovary, and both Dr Di Luzio and Dr Forsythe agree with me that they'll be very interested to see how this one turns out.'

'Hang on a minute. Dr Forsythe?' The name was familiar, and Nell's casual use of it distracted her from Alison Scanlon's details for the moment.

'Yes,' Nell answered crisply. 'He's...' She hesitated for a tell-tale moment. 'New in the department. Started today, in fact.'

'*Bren* Forsythe, we're talking about? Bren from years ago, Nell? Or someone else?'

'Yes, Bren Forsythe.' Nell's tone was even more businesslike. 'He's back. Our new general surgeon.'

Caroline wasn't fooled by the tone for one instant, but she swallowed further questions for the moment. 'Tell me about Alison Scanlon,' she said, then added innocently, 'But first, are you free for lunch?'

Nell wasn't so easily fooled. 'How much is lunch going to cost me?' she drawled, and Caroline knew she wasn't talking money.

'Nothing, unless you want it to,' she said.

'All right, and I probably won't want to. There's really...nothing to say, Caroline. Honestly. He's back. That's all. Twelve-thirty? Café? I've only got half an hour.'

'See you there. Now, tell me the bottom line on the biopsy, and I'll get Declan so he can hear the details.'

'No bottom line yet, until he's looked at what we took out, but it does look, cautiously, better than we feared. Three people are calling me, Caro, so—'

Caroline got Declan to the phone in five seconds, with four words. 'Nell. Alison Scanlon's biopsy.'

The two doctors had a short, technical conversation which Caroline couldn't hear from her desk, then Declan came back. 'What did Nell tell you, Caroline?' he asked.

'Not much, but I want to hear.'

Natalia looked interested, too, as she'd heard about the tragic case.

'The tumour has shrunk remarkably after the treatment. They're sending up the sample, and I'll do the lab work on it myself so we can see it under the microscope this afternoon. Meanwhile, guess what Gian Di Luzio found inside the lump on the ovary, once they'd removed it?'

'Not a clue, Declan.'

'A tooth, and some hair.'

'Eww!' Natalia made a face. 'Don't tell me things like that!'

'All right, so it does sound weird,' he agreed, 'but it's not all that uncommon, and it's great news.'

He spoke quickly, and his eyes were bright. Seeing him like this, Caroline realised he'd looked tired and preoccupied all morning. She had instinctively trodden carefully with him. She'd kept her distance, limited her conversation, and she hadn't even known she'd been doing it until now, when she recognised the way his mood had changed.

'It means the lump in the ovary isn't a secondary tumour,' he said, 'but almost certainly a benign dermoid cyst, containing multi-potential tissue.'

'Multi-potential,' Natalia repeated, in her strong accent.

'Tissue that can grow into anything—like teeth and hair—but isn't malignant or dangerous in any way. When I first heard about the lump on the ovary, it seemed to confirm that everything we feared about the breast was true.'

'But if the ovary is a benign, unrelated condition...' Caroline came in.

'Exactly. It's possible the cancer hasn't spread, and since the breast tumour has responded so well to treatment...' He paced the office. 'Lord, I never thought this woman had the palest ghost of a chance, but now just maybe...' he closed his forefinger and thumb together, leaving the tiniest slit of space between them '...maybe she does.'

At the hospital café two hours later, Caroline found Nell already seated by the window, unwrapping a sensible chicken salad sandwich from its plastic covering. She had a cup of tea and a banana, too, the rotten woman! Under such circumstances, Caroline couldn't possibly get a big, triangular piece of the chocolate walnut cake she coveted.

Joining Nell, with her own toasted cheese and tomato sandwich, strawberry yoghurt and hot chocolate, Caroline tried without success to read her friend's face.

Nell was an expert in the art of masking her feelings behind a terrifyingly cool façade. Her nickname in her own department was IQ, which stood for Ice Queen as well as being a pointer to her bright mind. Most of her staff bought the façade without question, and Nell was apparently very satisfied with her own professional image.

Old friends such as Emma Croft and Caroline herself weren't fooled, but they didn't challenge Nell on the issue very often, all the same. Caroline suspected that Nell had something to protect, or something to hide, and she'd always wondered if that something had anything to do with Bren Forsythe.

During Nell and Caroline's final year of high school, Bren had been the top student at Ranleigh, the local private boys' school where Caroline wanted to send Josh next year. Nell had occupied the same top position at Ranleigh's sister school, Glenfallon Ladies'

College. She and Bren had gone out together for a few months during that unique, tumultuous window of time around final exams and Christmas and the wait for results in January, when everyone's life had been up in the air and everything had seemed terribly, wonderfully important.

Even then, Nell had been fairly private about it. Caroline hadn't known, at the time, if this had been because the relationship had been desperately serious or because it hadn't been serious at all. Bren had had some health problems, she remembered, but she hadn't ever known what they were or whether they'd been significant.

Then, even though Nell, Caroline and Bren had all been studying medicine, they'd each gone their separate ways for a time. Caroline had been accepted into Sydney University, where she'd met Robert, Nell had chosen Newcastle, and Bren had moved to Melbourne, where he'd deferred his studies for a year.

Nell had always planned to return to Glenfallon. 'To protect Dad from Mum,' she'd said, in that cryptic way she had. Joking? Or not?

As she'd outlined to Declan weeks ago, Caroline had limped back here with a failed marriage and a failed medical career. It had seemed like a backward step at the time. Not any more. She loved it here now.

Bren hadn't come back at all, not even for holidays, as his family had moved to Melbourne, too, at the same time. Seventeen years on, Caroline would have assumed him to be totally set up in his career, with a wife and children, and probably a golf club membership and various other professional accoutrements as well. If his return to Glenfallon was going to haunt her best friend, she wasn't happy about it.

'So…' she said, then mentally scored herself zero points for this brilliant conversational opener.

'You didn't get cake?' Nell looked disappointed at the items on Caroline's tray. 'I was planning to con you into giving me half.'

'By mentioning my diet, right? I saw your banana and felt too guilty.'

'Then the banana backfired completely.'

'We were supposed to share the banana as an antidote to cake poison?'

'I won't try to be so clever next time.'

Caroline decided not to try to be clever either. 'Tell me about Bren,' she said simply.

'There's nothing to tell. He was ready for a change. He knew we were likely to need someone. We always need someone, if they're good, and of course he is.'

'So you must have known for a while?'

'A few weeks, yes.' Nell looked up, tried to meet Caroline's eyes and failed. This was unusual.

'Why didn't you say anything?'

'Say what? That the hospital board had hired him? It might have fallen through. And, Caroline, please don't start—' She broke off, and began again. 'Seventeen years is a long time.' She laughed. The sound cut and twisted in the air. Nell's laugh had always been a complicated thing. 'If I'd been in any doubt about that, one look at him proved the point.'

'Why? Has he aged?'

'No! I have!'

'Not badly, Nell. Most people wouldn't think you were thirty-five.'

'Hmm. From a few of the looks he given me, he's not most people. Anyhow, tell me if your car's running properly now after you had to mortgage your first-born to pay for the repairs, tell me the latest news on your sister-in-law, and tell me what Declan said about Alison Scanlon.'

'You're changing the subject, Nell.'

'That's right. I am. Live with it.'

Caroline considered pushing further, but decided not to. 'The car seems fine. They fixed the oil leak, said I'd been very lucky. No visible damage to the engine, but I'm to keep my eye on it. Sandie's having her second cycle of treatment in Canberra this week, and she felt wretched after it last time, so she's not looking forward to it. As for Alison Scanlon's biopsy, Declan is going to do the lab preparation work himself,' she said. 'He's in such a hurry to see it.'

'Tell him to phone me, or phone me yourself, as soon as he has a diagnosis, because I'm in a hurry, too. After seeing her breast that day six and a half weeks ago, if she's going to live, I want to be one of the first to know. I liked her. I was absolutely furious with her, but I liked her.' Nell's face went still and thoughtful. 'We had a couple of things in common, I think.'

*   *   *

As soon as Alison's pathology arrived in the department, Declan put the rest of his workload on hold and went along to the lab.

'I'm going to section this one myself,' he told lab technician, Mary Bennett. 'Will you get it ready for me?'

'You won't get to it today,' she warned.

'I know. First thing tomorrow, I hope.'

The tissue sample required several steps in processing before he could even begin to cut and stain it. It would be cut to a specific size, dehydrated and embedded in paraffin, so that the knife blade could make clean cuts and produce thin enough cross-sections.

Tomorrow, it would probably take him an hour to complete the preparation of the tissue for analysis. He felt a need to hurry the process, but knew that such impatience could seriously compromise an accurate result.

'This is the Scanlon case?' Mary asked.

For some reason, the entire department wanted the result on this one. It wasn't by any means the only life-or-death case they'd worked on recently, but they'd all come to care about the outcome. With her husband a science teacher at the local high school, and primary school-aged children of her own, Mary must be around Alison's age.

'Yes, it is,' Declan confirmed. 'Do you know her?'

'Not personally, but my sister-in-law works with her sister.'

'The kind of connection you get in this town, I'm finding.'

'Makes it hard sometimes.'

'Makes it rewarding, too.'

Declan got into work early the next morning, when only one of the lab technicians, Julianne, had begun work. 'It's ready,' she told him, and pointed. 'Over on the bench.'

'Thanks. It looks good so far.'

He sectioned the entire sample, having to force himself to use the big blade carefully as he carved each wafer-thin slice. His back began to ache and his eyes already felt tired and gritty, but he forced his concentration to stay sharp and focused.

He hadn't had anywhere near enough sleep this weekend, with Suzy down. She'd deprived him of sleep many times in the past, but on this occasion he couldn't say that he'd found much in compensation, either before their talk or after it.

He had a lot to think about now that she'd gone back to Sydney.

Not now, though. Now he had to think about the work in front of him.

With every cut of the wax-encased block of tissue, he looked for evidence of the tumour in the tissue's architecture, and with every cut he couldn't find it. That didn't mean very much. His diagnosis would be made on the basis of what he saw beneath the microscope, not with the naked eye.

He ended up with fifty blocks of tissue set on fifty slides, each sample transparently thin, measuring approximately one and a half centimetres square and stained the familiar pinkish-purple. With the tissue's architecture still in place, these slides would look very different to the pap smears and sputum samples he so often saw. They'd have the appearance of maps, or photographs of landscapes, taken from space.

With his office door closed, he set the slide trays beside his computer, switched on his microscope and brought the case details up on screen. In the background, he heard the department slowly come to life. Steph would be at the reception desk by now, her eyes bright and ready to appreciate a joke behind the tiny frames of her glasses. Tom would be checking his e-mails. The lab technicians might already have received a case or two from today's surgery.

It was a quarter to nine. Caroline wouldn't get here for another twenty minutes, after delivering her son and her nephews to child-care and school.

OK, so, Scanlon, Alison.

He slid in the first slide and focused the microscope to begin his painstaking study of all fifty cross-sections. At first, he couldn't find any evidence of a tumour at all. Was it possible that Alison's chemotherapy had shrunk it away completely? Then, as the cross-sections he studied grew closer to the centre of the excised tissue, he began to understand what he was seeing.

This wasn't the carcinoma that he'd been so sure he'd find, but a sarcoma.

Yes, it was cancer, but it hadn't metastasised, and it probably wouldn't. It wasn't the type of cancer that did. Nell Cassidy and Bren Forsythe had completely excised the shrunken tumour during surgery. There was no evidence of abnormality at any of the margins. He'd never expected to find himself looking at something this good.

He stood up, looked at his watch. Almost ten. Only now did he feel a knob of his spine burning near the top of his back. He'd been so focused on this. He stretched, rolled his neck and shoulders and opened his door.

Across the corridor, Caroline and Natalia were both at work. He paused for a moment before he spoke, and watched Caroline's concentration as she made a dab of blue on the slide she was studying.

She had her hair up in a clip and he could see her neck and the delicate shading of the downy tendrils that had escaped. The sight reminded him of the day he'd brought Pete Croft home with a sprained ankle several weeks ago, to find the massage session in progress. He'd felt like a voyeur, watching Caroline's naked, oiled back. It was crazy to feel the same way here at work.

And yet he really needed to keep his distance from her now, even more than he had needed to that day six and a half weeks ago. She'd pick up on it, he knew, and she would be hurt, but that couldn't be helped. The last thing he wanted was to get any closer to her right now. He needed to wait, and he needed to think.

'Natalia?' he said, deliberately using her name first. 'Or Caroline?'

Both women looked up.

'If I want to send something to a different lab for a second opinion, what's the procedure? Is there a particular lab we'd choose?'

'Westmead,' Natalia said.

'What is it?' Caroline asked.

'Alison Scanlon.'

She made a pained face, and nodded. 'Then, yes, we'd usually send it to Westmead. So you've found the tumour and identified it?'

'Yes.

'What's in doubt?'

'Nothing, really.'

'Oh.' Caroline's face fell.

Natalia had turned back to her microscope, but she gave a little nod, and Declan knew she was still listening.

'I just don't like the idea,' he said, 'of telling a patient that she's got her life back without a second opinion to back me up. I'm not sure that she could stand another reversal of fortune, and I want to be absolutely sure.'

'You mean...?'

'It's sarcoma, not carcinoma, and Nell and the new surgeon have got all of it out. The cells around the entire perimeter of the excision are normal to a measurement of ten millimetres. She has a really good prognosis and she should be fine.'

'That's wonderful!' Caroline said, blinking back tears. 'That's not what anyone expected a few weeks ago.'

'No, it isn't. It's great. I can't even imagine how she'll react to this.'

'Could we look at it?' Natalia asked.

'Yes, the trays are on my desk. Do you want to bring them in here? Put slide three into the multi-header, and I'll get Tom.'

Declan disappeared again, and Caroline heard him at Tom's open office door a few seconds later. Carefully, she put the blue-tipped toothpick back in her little bottle of artist's colour, not knowing quite why her hand felt so unsteady.

The news about Alison was great, almost miraculous. She couldn't treat it as any kind of omen for Sandie, but it felt like one all the same. Alison's case had seemed so hopeless, the worst possible punishment for her initial, long-lasting denial. Sandie's illness had been diagnosed far earlier, and the overall survival rate for Hodgkin's lymphoma was statistically much better than the survival rate for breast cancer. If Alison could 'get her life back', as Declan had phrased it, then surely Sandie could, too?

But Caroline knew that cancer didn't always work that way.

She wondered if Declan would guess how hard she had to fight to keep the two cases unconnected in her mind. He'd hardly spoken to her for the past couple of days, and she knew she hadn't just imagined the way he was keeping his distance.

One part of her felt wounded by it, and she could easily have asked him, 'What have I done? Have I offended you? Is something wrong?'

The rest of her knew how disastrous it would be if she blurted out those questions. She didn't need to ask them. She knew exactly why he'd stepped back from their easy office friendship.

He'd recognised how hard she had to fight to keep herself from imagining something much closer and deeper, something that could never happen because of his commitment elsewhere. She even thought that he wasn't immune to the awareness himself. It was one of those ships-that-pass-in-the-night things. In another life, they might have become involved. In this life, it was dangerous to even think about it.

She sat down at the multi-header, deliberately choosing the eyepiece closest to the window. Natalia brought in the slide trays and sat beside her, and Caroline was sure that Declan would choose the position opposite Natalia. He didn't, though. Striding in front of him, Tom gave him no choice. Out of habit, Tom took the control position and found the slide Natalia had already put in.

They spent nearly twenty minutes on the case, with Tom flicking knobs and arrows and Declan talking them through what he'd already seen—the margins clear of any sign of tumour, the evidence which distinguished this form of breast sarcoma from carcinoma.

Breast carcinomas arose from the lining cells of the ducts, while sarcoma came from tissue such as the smooth muscle which supported the lining cells. The two were very different, and the microscope made the differences clear. Carcinoma cells were large and round, while sarcoma cells were long and thin, and looked a little like worms.

Declan's voice seemed to fall on Caroline's skin like a caress, like the massage he'd once witnessed. She couldn't forget how close he was, couldn't stop herself from wishing he was closer, and hated herself for it. Not just because it was wrong, but because it was such a hopeless, doomed longing.

Why do I spend so much energy fighting the wrong battles? she wondered.

The round window of bright, patterned light blurred in her vision and she surrendered the chance to learn, which she would normally have seized on. She thought about how she'd fought that losing battle to pass third-year medicine after Josh's birth, instead of stepping back and deferring her studies for a year or two. She'd fought to keep her marriage alive for too long also. She'd tried to talk Robert into seeing a counsellor together even after he'd moved out.

Now she had another battle with Robert, sitting on a slow boil and currently going nowhere—the battle over Woodside. She had to make a decision soon. Concede? Or prepare herself for the realistic possibility of a court battle? Which would be least harmful to Josh?

Do I somehow make this stuff happen? she wondered. Or is it just bad luck?

She began the journey down a familiar road of self-doubt—a rutted, twisting road along which she seemed to recognise every pothole.

I'm not going down it again, she decided. Not over the Woodside thing, and not over Declan. I'm just not!

'Thanks, Declan,' Tom said, standing up. 'That was fascinating.'

'I'll call the surgeons, give them the news.'

'Nell Cassidy specifically asked to be told as soon as possible,' Caroline reported.

'Get Steph to arrange sending the slides to Westmead,' Tom said. 'I agree we want to be a hundred per cent certain on this one. Tell her GP what we're up to, because this will delay things by a few days.'

Everyone went back to work, energised by the positive outcome to what had seemed such a hopeless case. Between them, Natalia and Caroline emptied their in-tray by lunchtime, when Caroline normally left now to pick up Sam from child-care. The two of them stopped off to buy groceries, read a story over lunch, walked to the playground and went to pick up Mattie and Josh at three.

When the boys were settled with afternoon snacks and a children's show on the television, Caroline sat herself down, picked up the phone, took a deep breath and dialled her ex-husband's home number.

She wanted to talk to Gail.

'He never asked me about it, Caroline,' Gail said.

'He seemed to feel it would be unfair to you, and to Amelia. Maybe he didn't want to put you in the position of being cast as the wicked stepmother if you felt you had to say no.'

'Unfair to me, I can understand. Although I don't feel that way, and he should have known that. I'd love to have Josh living with us during school terms. As for Amelia, she adores her big brother. Robert is over-protective of her, and of me, but he can't see it.' She sighed, then laughed fondly.

'Oh, I'm glad you can, though. He actually suggested...' Caroline began.

Then she stopped. Gail obviously had no idea that Robert feared Josh might bully his baby sister, or worse, and from what she'd already said, she wouldn't think highly of such fears. The two of them had a good marriage. For all sorts of reasons, it would be better for Caroline to keep Robert's words to herself. She quickly manufactured an entirely new ending to her sentence.

'Suggested, well, that if I happened to get married again to the right sort of man, who'd provide more of a positive male influence for Josh, he'd look at the situation differently. That's somewhat over-protective, in my opinion.'

'I love him for it, but I'm not going to let him get away with it,' Gail concluded. 'We'll talk about it tonight, and I'll tell him how much Amelia and I would love Josh living with us. Don't worry, Caroline. I absolutely understand your qualms about him boarding at Woodside, and I'm sure I can talk Robert round.'

'Th-thank you, Gail. I really appreciate it. This has been tying me in knots for a while.'

'You'll still miss him, though, won't you?' the other woman suggested gently.

'Oh, too much to express.' Her throat tightened. 'But at least I won't worry so much.' It seemed like the best compromise she could hope for, and she had to learn not to fight those losing battles she'd spent herself on in the past.

'And I'll work on the rugby thing, too, after I've bided my time a bit,' Gail said.

'The rugby thing?'

'I could see Josh didn't enjoy the coaching weekend.'

'Could you? Oh, I'm so glad.' This was more than Caroline had dared to hope for. If Gail had the perception about Josh that Robert lacked, she would breathe so much easier.

'Robert could see it, too, but he's not quite ready to give up yet. He has such high hopes for Josh, Caroline, and he's so proud of him, even if he shows it in all the wrong ways sometimes.'

And that's why Gail and Robert are happy together, when Robert and I never were, Caroline thought after she'd put down the phone. Gail finds the best in him.

CHAPTER EIGHT

IN THE northern hemisphere, today would have been the summer solstice—the lightest day of the year. In Australia, it was the winter solstice, but Declan couldn't take the season seriously at all when it came in a package like this. Crisp nights, mild and sunny days, an occasional bite of wind, and none of the rain that everyone in the district, farmer or not, would have celebrated.

It was more than six weeks since he'd ended his relationship with Suzy. Six whole weeks. Nobody in Glenfallon knew about it yet, and didn't it damn the whole nature of the relationship that he could quietly shift his entire future and say nothing about it, without causing a ripple of comment or awareness?

He'd spent a weekend in Sydney at the end of May, but he and Suzy hadn't seen each other. Instead, he'd taken a hotel room at Darling Harbour and soaked up the city on his own, trying to work out what he wanted, why he'd let this whole mess happen in the first place. He'd reached certain conclusions, but he hadn't tested their validity as yet, and he didn't know what his conclusions told him about the future.

Should he plan on going back to London as soon as Tom Robinson could find a replacement for him? Tom was attending a conference this week, and hoped to get someone interested in taking over his own position when he retired. Declan could speak frankly to him, suggest that he should be on the lookout for two people.

There was no reason, on paper, for him to stay in Glenfallon. Even if he didn't return to London, it would surely make more sense to sit those Australian exams, a year or so from now, and build a life in Sydney.

He understood, now, that he hadn't loved Suzy and she hadn't loved him. Or not by any useful, meaningful definition of the word 'love' anyway. He'd talked to Caroline, weeks ago, about what it was like to be a middle child in a large, poor family—how you grabbed what was on offer before you'd worked out if you wanted it or not.

He'd done that with Suzy. She'd offered. Herself, and then Sydney. He'd grabbed. He'd discovered too late that he didn't want what he'd only ever half held in his hands, in any case.

He remembered how he'd planned, back in April, to tell Suzy that he'd 'consider' marriage if she would meet him halfway, if she'd give a little more, if she'd make a commitment to more than simply having fun together.

Crazy! A man shouldn't 'consider' marriage. The word was just wrong. Having seen his parents happy together for forty years despite his father's weaknesses and his mother's blind spots, he believed in love. He just didn't know quite how he'd recognise it if it happened.

As soon as he had realised that what he felt for Suzy most definitely *wasn't* love, he hadn't wanted to be with her any more, even if what their relationship had offered in the short term was as good as it had ever been. He'd tried to break the news without hurting her. Had he succeeded? Hard to know.

She'd reacted angrily. 'Because I didn't smile in the right way at your cancer case in the supermarket yesterday morning?'

'No, but—'

'That's ridiculous, Dec.'

Maybe it was. He'd managed to articulate some more of what he felt, resorting to a poetic, Irish whimsicality of phrasing that she didn't appreciate. Stuff about the high noon of your life, and the twilight, about two kinds of magic, and the kind that faded first. He didn't really know what he was trying to say. Lucky she was the writer, not he.

Then it turned out that she had a heavy flirtation going on with one of the other writers working on the TV mini-series. 'I should have slept with him after all, instead of pulling it to a screaming halt and leaving both of us frustrated as hell. Why I thought it was necessary to have any scruples about fidelity, I don't know!'

'If you think fidelity is about getting to the brink in another man's arms before the scruples kick in, then your definition of the word is very different to mine!' he retorted, and things got pretty nasty after that.

She stormed off. They hadn't talked since. He'd wanted to go to Sydney just to prove that the woman and the city...or the whole country...didn't have to stay linked in his mind. This place had other things to offer without

Suzy. This time he had to work out exactly what he really wanted before he grabbed.

It was two in the afternoon now. The short day, a Monday, had already tipped past its zenith and into its slide towards dusk at around five o'clock. He stretched at his desk, heard a crack or two in his spine and shoulder joints. Wooden slide trays still sat piled up beside him, and he'd promised to tackle a post-mortem for Tom this afternoon. Meanwhile, Natalia would be expecting him across the corridor soon to review any abnormal Paps, urines and sputums she and Caroline had come across since yesterday.

He left his desk, but instead of seeing Natalia when he pushed open the cyto technicians' office door he found Caroline, and he couldn't stop the rush of pleasure he felt. She looked good. A little tired, maybe, with all the extra work she was putting in, caring for her nephews. But still good.

And she made him feel good, too, the same kind of good he felt in the evening after a long day, when he sat down with a glass of wine, music on the CD player, a hot curry from the House of Siam and a page-turning book—content, replete, relaxed, expectant, just *good*.

Hiding it, as he'd been hiding it for six weeks and more, he asked her, 'Not with the boys today?'

Smiling slightly, she answered, 'I'll have to leave just before three to pick them up, but Natalia had another commitment and we would have slipped behind if I hadn't filled in for her. Sam's staying on at child-care for an extra two hours. They'll be going back to the farm on the weekend. Sandie's giving herself the week to recover from her third treatment cycle, but she's insisting she'll be strong enough to see them by Friday. As usual, she's desperate to be with them again.'

'I'm sorry the treatment is giving her such a rough time.'

'And she has three more cycles still to come.'

'Are there any signs that she's responding?'

'Her nodes have gone down.'

'That's good. That's the most concrete thing you can hope for at this stage. Much for us to look at here?'

'A few things.'

He saw that she'd already filled in the sheet that recorded their sessions at the multi-header, and the reason for them. 'Review abnormals' was the most common notation, and that was what she'd written today. She'd put down her initials in the attendance column, and he added his own with a quick scrawl. When the session was finished, she'd note the amount of time they'd spent.

She sat down opposite the control position and gave him the first slide. Their fingers touched, and his surging physical reaction to her mere presence and to this tiny flicker of contact told him he couldn't keep up his careful façade for much longer. Maybe it was time to let it go, in any case.

For the past six weeks, he'd needed it as a protection for both of them. He didn't want to hurt her, and he didn't want to make another mistake like Suzy. You reached a point, however, where you couldn't know what you wanted, or how deep something might go, unless you took the risk of trying it, making it real. He'd already hurt Caroline by backing off so much from their initial friendship. It didn't make sense to wait any longer.

Moving the lens across different sections of the slide, he found the dot of white she'd placed to the left of the group of abnormal cells.

'Yes, stop there. Those are the cells I didn't like,' she said.

'OK,' he murmured. Her knees were directly opposite his, clothed in a swish of navy skirt fabric.

He focused his gaze more accurately through the eye-piece. Under the microscope, that tiny, delicate dab of white he'd seen her place on so many slides over the past three months looked like a big grey blob, and just to the right of it he could see exactly which cells had concerned her. They both studied the untidy cluster in silence for a moment.

'Yes, they're atypical,' he agreed. 'Not quite clear what they are.'

'No, nothing to panic about.'

'But definitely not right.'

'And this test is a follow-up twelve months after she had the same result on her previous test,' Caroline pointed out.

'You're suggesting I recommend she sees a gynaecologist?'

'With two results like this in a year, yes.'

'I'd agree. It may be hormonal changes that need to be looked at.'

Caroline moved the lens to a different section of the slide. 'This area looked atrophic, to my eye.'

'Again, yes, I'd agree. More evidence that it's secondary to hormonal changes. Anything else on this one?'

'No, but this next one's more serious, I think. I'd report it as CIN 3.' She used the shorthand they were both familiar with. It stood for cervical intraepithelial neoplasia, grade three, and no one wanted to utter that mouthful any more often than they had to.

The slide came into view, full of pink and purple washes of colour, draped like chiffon scarves across the circular golden light. Again, the dots she'd placed beside more than one group of cells showed as opaque grey blobs.

Looking at the cells, he had to agree with her. There was strong evidence on this slide of high-grade abnormality in the skin layer of the cervix. If this patient had been having regular normal smears until now, as her records showed that she had, the cancer should be pre-invasive, treatable and curable. There were several options for treatment, including freezing, burning or surgical incision.

The real problems came when women avoided seeing their doctors for the test, because an abnormality like this could progress, if untreated, to squamous cell carcinoma of the cervix. A 'silent' condition until well advanced, it was usually fatal.

'I'll recommend a colposcopy and biopsy.' He knew by this time that the colposcopy procedure could be done in Glenfallon, probably by Gian Di Luzio, and that the biopsy samples would be sent here for analysis. Further treatment would be dictated by what his own study of the cells revealed.

'And this last one?' They both lifted their heads from the microscope and she passed another slide across.

Their fingers touched again. Deliberately, Declan let the contact continue for just a fraction of a second longer than it should have, and saw Caroline's eyes dart to his face then drop quickly.

'Sorry,' she said, as if she thought it was her fault. 'I've been a bit clumsy today. Sam had me up twice in the night, and I'm tired.'

'Don't apologise,' he said, and she looked at him in alarm once again, hearing the caress he'd put into his voice. 'You're always blaming yourself.'

'Can we look at the slide?' she asked. 'I'll have to go soon.'

'My turn to apologise?' he suggested. He'd certainly destroyed the relaxed yet focused atmosphere between them in this quiet office, with only the hum of the computer as background noise.

'No, not at all.' She took a breath, changed her tone quickly. 'This one seemed pretty clear to me. HPV.'

Again, he understood the medical shorthand at once. Human papilloma virus. It was a condition that could predispose the cervix to developing pre-cancerous cells, which in turn could progress to a more serious cell abnormality. He focused on the cell cluster she'd highlighted, and found the distinctive enlarged atypical cells.

'Three out of three. That's it, then?'

'Yes, fortunately.'

She seemed flustered, or even annoyed...yes, definitely annoyed...and he realised that he was going about this all wrong. They weren't teenagers, with no histories and no baggage, who could let looks and accidental touches progress effortlessly to the next stage.

Before he even knew for sure that she was interested, he had to let her know, with no ambiguity, that he was free to explore all the places their feelings might take them.

'Oh! Declan! It's you!' Caroline exclaimed at her front door the same evening. She'd changed from her uniform into jeans and a long-sleeved cotton top in a soft orange-pink, and her hair was half out of its clip. He doubted she'd noticed. She looked like a busy mother on a school night—flushed, alert, tired, loving and loved.

'A welcome fit to warm an Irishman's heart,' he said, teasing her with the exaggerated brogue.

'Well, it's...' she cocked her head, listened to the news headlines coming from the television '...seven o'clock. All right, no. Not late.'

'Have you eaten?'

'Yes, an hour ago. It works best with the boys. Oh, what have you brought?'

He held up the hot plastic bag of containers from the House of Siam. 'Dinner for two. Tell me you just had fish fingers, and you're hungry enough to join me.'

She flushed. 'I did. You're psychic. They love fish fingers. I'm not going to join you, though. Declan—'

'Listen, you're a hard woman to catch alone these days, but I want to talk to you. Apparently you can't be bribed by the smell of Thai chilli and noodles.'

'Um…'

He loved how flustered she looked. He loved the particular kind of flustered she looked, and hoped very strenuously that he'd interpreted it in the right way. Her sense of honour was locked in battle with her sense of the pull between them. He was sure he could end that battle pretty fast with the right words.

'Let me in for five minutes,' he said. 'I won't even unpack the containers. I've got something to say, and it's actually pretty simple.'

'Um, all right…' She stepped back, holding the door, and he came inside. They both glanced into the lounge-room and saw that the boys had grabbed the remote control to bring up a sit com on another channel. 'This once, Josh,' she warned her son, raising her voice to get his attention. 'Seven o'clock television is not suddenly an iron-clad tradition in this house, OK?'

'OK, Mum.'

'Harder when it gets dark early,' Declan said.

'You're right.' She gave a short nod. 'In summer, I'd send them outside.'

He'd only seen her front hall until now, the day she'd phoned needing an emergency lift to Sydney. This time she took him to the back, where an original rear porch had been enclosed to make a small family room, and a wall had been knocked down to connect it with the kitchen.

The renovation wasn't as ambitious or extensive as the one at her parents' house, but it created a nice atmosphere all the same, with a colour scheme of soft creamy yellow and smoky blue. He imagined she had a mortgage that would hang over her for a number of years yet.

'Can I put these in the kitchen?' he asked.

Watching him do so before she'd told him he could, Caroline wondered what on earth was happening here. He'd given her six weeks of distance and stiffness since shortly after their trip to Sydney. She'd reached the point where his teasing request for an ally in the department, when he'd first started, just seemed like an embarrassing memory. Now he'd shown up on her doorstep with no warning, carrying a load of steaming food.

He was right. Her stomach couldn't be bought or bribed.

'You've got something to say,' she reminded him.

He leaned his forearms on the benchtop, beside the plastic bag he'd put there, and pinned her feet to the floor with his steady gaze. 'Suzy and I have split up,' he said.

Her legs went wobbly, and the wrong word came out. 'Why?'

'Short answer? I discovered that I didn't love her, and she didn't seem to care. All for the best.'

'That's the short answer all right,' she agreed. The wobbliness climbed higher, and reached her lungs. Her words came out choppy and in the wrong order. 'Insultingly short almost. So you're leaving, that means?'

'Leaving?'

'Leaving Glenfallon,' she said. 'Going back to England.'

She knew he'd only taken two years leave of absence from his permanent position in London. He'd burned no boats, like her parents with their Gold Coast experiment. Sensibly, in her parents' case. They were planning to come back here. Sandie's illness had made them realise that they didn't want to be so far from family.

Meanwhile, Declan would return to London.

'No!' he said, his mouth making the word into a pout of protest beneath a heavy frown. 'At least...' He took a breath. 'No, that's not what I wanted to tell you.'

'Tom will be relieved,' she said thinly.

'Make this a bit easier, Caroline.'

'How? I'm— OK. Thank you for telling me about you and Suzy.' She couldn't think straight. Did he want to back out of his lease? Mum and Dad wouldn't mind that. She gathered her wits and ploughed on. 'Uh...she was here for the weekend, I suppose. I'm sure it was hard, even though—'

'It happened six weeks ago.'

'Six weeks!'

It seemed like such a long time, because so much had happened.

Autumn had turned to winter. Nell Cassidy's old flame, Bren Forsythe, had come back to town to work at the hospital. Alison Scanlon had been given her miraculous news. Caroline had had that important talk over the phone with Gail. Mum and Dad had made a visit. Sandie had reached the halfway point in her treatment, and was showing signs of the right response, but there was still a long way to go.

Declan had barely spoken to Caroline during all of this, and she'd blamed herself.

Today, thinking back, six weeks felt like forever.

'I didn't want to say anything until we'd both had a cushion of time, for a little protection,' he said.

'You and Suzy?'

'You and me, Caroline.'

'You and me?'

He stayed silent for a moment, straightened carefully from leaning on the bench, watching her. 'Have I been reading you wrongly all this time, then?' he finally said.

'I haven't angled for you and Suzy to split up. At no point have I done that! Tom's been...practically praying for it, and if it had ever occurred to him at any point that I might be—' She stopped.

Apparently she didn't need wine or hypnotic highways or any external stimulus at all when it came to spilling blunt truths to this man.

'Might be what?' Declan said. He hadn't taken his eyes from her face.

'Interested,' she answered, after racking her brains for a better word, a less *out there* word. She couldn't find one.

'And are you?'

'Ah-h...' What was that? Sigh? Moan?

He'd left the bench. He was coming closer. She discovered that she'd taken a step in his direction as well. She could touch him if she held out her hands. 'Are you interested, Caroline?'

'Yes!' she answered wildly. 'Of course I am. You know I am. Isn't that why you backed off? You knew how I felt.'

'I hoped,' he corrected. 'I didn't know.'

'Good! That's better than I feared!'

'You wouldn't let it show, and I wouldn't let it get important—'

'I couldn't help that,' she cut in. 'It got important no matter how hard I tried.'

'Because of the mess with Suzy. You're right. It got important no matter how hard I tried. Six weeks isn't long.'

'It is. It was. It felt long.'

'I hope it's long enough for me to have drawn the right conclusions as to how I could have made such a mistake.'

'With Suzy.'

'Yes. Definitely the mistake was with Suzy. And six weeks was necessary. Minimal, in fact.'

'Do you want longer?' she offered, hardly knowing what she'd said. 'Because if—'

'No. I do not want longer.' He reached her, and wrapped his arms around her waist, looking down into her face with eyes like the sun on the sea. 'I do not want one second longer, Caroline.'

'Declan…'

Desire and need slammed into her like a gust of hot north wind, like gravity after weightlessness. She melted inside, and couldn't say another word. Her mouth felt numb and incredibly sensitised at the same time. Knowing he would kiss her within seconds, she let her lips sigh apart. She felt dizzy with the suddenness of this, and with how right it felt.

'Well, do you?' He pulled her closer. So close, from her breasts to her thighs. His body felt hot, hard, expectant, wonderful. 'After what's happened, I have to offer you that. Do you want longer?'

'No,' she said, and lifted her face to meet his mouth. 'Not one second longer.'

They tasted each other, taking it slowly, sharing a sense of wonder and delight that this was actually happening, and real. All sorts of things clicked into place. All those times when their eyes had met, sharing an unspoken joke. The sensation she always had when they were alone together that she'd just drunk a glass of wine on an empty stomach, even when she hadn't. The way they'd talked in the car on the journey back from Sydney.

Caroline closed her eyes and put all of it, everything she'd felt and felt now and could feel so much deeper, into the press of her mouth on his. She let her tongue tease him and her breath sigh over his face. She ran her hands up his muscular back, up the warm, lightly tanned curve of his neck that she'd wanted to touch for so long, and into the soft prickle of his hair.

And she didn't let herself think for one second about his very temporary commitment to her home town.

'You kiss so sweetly,' he murmured.

'You taste good. The way you talk...tastes good.'

'The way I talk?' He pulled back a little, brushed the tips of his fingers across her mouth and smiled. 'That has a taste?'

'Irish whiskey.' She tried to imitate him, but couldn't. She laughed. 'Even that first day on the phone...do you remember, when I thought you'd be Josh...your voice curled out of the phone into my ear and made me feel that we knew each other.'

'Mmm, I know. I kept thinking I could make that feeling between us go away if Suzy would just spend more time— But I don't want to talk about her. She's gone. She's happy.'

'Is she?'

'Jumped into bed with someone else. Was more than halfway there, it turned out, while I was still whipping myself for looking at you in the wrong way.'

'I would never have responded to—'

'No, neither would I. Neither would I, Caroline.'

Her name got lost in their kiss. She held his hips, and felt so soft and full with need that she almost thought she might fall if she let him go. She could have clawed his clothes from his body, branded every inch of his skin with her mouth, clung to him all night.

'What're we going to do about this, sweetheart?' he said. 'The boys are in the other room.'

'The weekend. Sandie and Chris want to have Josh out at the farm. My calendar is...pretty open.'

So is my heart. After all these weeks, I'm not exactly playing hard to get, and you'd be pretty unaware, Declan, if you didn't notice.

Did it matter?

She couldn't even consider the question. After blaming herself, these past six weeks, for his distance— She'd scared him off, hadn't she? She'd been obvious, pitiable. Or so her thoughts had run—she couldn't pretend, now, to a coolness she didn't possess. Especially when he didn't seem to want her to be cool at all.

'Like the sound of that,' he said, brushing her mouth with the words. 'Shall I turn up here after work?'

'Chris is coming in to pick up the boys straight after school. Yes, that'd be fine.' She'd cook something nice. She'd have wine chilled. That was plenty to plan. The rest could stay open-ended. 'I'm collecting Josh Sunday afternoon.'

'I'll share the driving with you, if you want. Is there a place we could stop for a picnic on the way?'

'A few places.'

'If we don't sleep in too late.'

'Uh, yes, that could be a problem.' She felt the colour rise in her cheeks, and heat seep into her bones.

'Auntie Caroline?' came an urgent, indignant voice from the other room.

'Yes, love?' she answered Sam.

Declan let her go, trailing his fingers down her arms, bringing every hair to attention.

'Mattie's sitting on me, and he won't get off,' Sam yelled.

'Sounds like an emergency,' Declan murmured.

'Are you staying to eat that Thai chilli?'

'Am I invited?'

'You brought the food.' She laughed, stopped fighting her losing battle, flung her caution into the air like a handful of sand in the wind. She couldn't think about Declan's future plans yet, or she'd ruin what they had so suddenly and wonderfully found in the present. 'Yes, Declan,' she said. 'You're invited. Even though you don't need an invitation.'

'What time do they go to bed?'

'Too late tonight,' she whispered, 'for what we're both thinking of.'

CHAPTER NINE

'SHE'S Indian, trained partially there and partially in Britain, but her husband's Australian,' Tom said, sounding excited.

He'd arrived back from his conference in Sydney that afternoon, and had dropped in to check on things before the weekend. Declan was ready to leave for the day, but Tom had cornered him and he couldn't be rude to a man he liked and respected, even though Tom's ways irked him at times.

'Like you,' the older man went on, 'she has another year or more before she can take our local exams. They're definitely committed to this country, though, and they're prepared to look widely for the best place to settle. Her husband's looking for an accountancy practice to buy into. He's apparently pretty flexible.'

'It sounds very promising, Tom,' Declan answered.

'You'd head up the department, since you've been here longer. That's if...' Tom stopped and scratched his head, looking as if he suspected he'd put his foot in his mouth. 'Is there any...?' He stopped once more.

'Tom, if you're asking how my future's shaping up,' Declan said reluctantly, 'I'm sorry, I don't have an answer on that for you. Not right now.'

'Suzy may find her novel takes longer to finish than she thought it would.'

'Suzy and I have split up.' He hadn't planned a general announcement yet, but he couldn't hedge or lie to Tom.

'Oh. Sorry to hear it.'

'It was mutual. Amicable.' More or less. 'And for the best. Don't be sorry.'

'It...uh...leaves your future a little more open-ended.'

'But not something you should count on, from your own perspective, Tom,' he said firmly.

He couldn't afford to let himself get backed into any corners by a rash promise made to someone he'd hate to disappoint. If there was any possibility of him staying on in Glenfallon, he should play it down to Tom, not build it up. And what about Caroline? Should he play it down to her, too? Or should he hint at a commitment he was by no means sure of yet? Neither choice seemed like the right one.

'London makes the most sense for me,' he told Tom slowly. 'My job will still be waiting for me there eighteen months from now.'

And Caroline would be waiting for him right now. If Tom kept him much longer, he'd be later than he'd promised.

'Of course,' the senior pathologist said. He couldn't hide his crestfallen face. 'Well, we'll be grateful for you for as long as we have you,' he added, his tone too hearty.

'Yes. But I mustn't keep you, Tom. You'll want to check your messages, and I need to get away.'

He left the building five minutes later, in the chilly winter dusk, with their conversation still hanging behind him like a dark cloud. It sounded warning bells, but the anticipation he felt about seeing Caroline had drowned out the bells by the time he reached her house.

She met him at the door, and in her expectant, slightly on edge mood and manner he saw his own state of mind reflected. She'd changed into stretch black trousers and a clingy sweater made of dark blue angora, and if she wore anything beneath the sweater but a bra, it didn't show.

He should have changed too, he realised, stopped at home rather than coming straight here, even if it meant being a little late. He should have brought wine, and definitely flowers. He usually had more finesse but, admit it, he'd been so impatient to see her, so distracted by his visions of their evening.

The first of how many?

He didn't yet know.

This was new, the way his relationship with Suzy had once been.

'Sorry I'm a bit late,' he said, shifting his weight on the front step. They didn't kiss or touch. Not yet. It would happen soon.

'That's fine,' she answered. 'Chris was a bit late getting the boys out of here. I'm still cooking.'

'Mmm, I can tell.' She had a tiny fragment of green on her cheek, just near her mouth. It looked like an eighteenth-century beauty spot, and arrowed his attention to her glossy lips. He stepped closer, brushed the herb fragment off with the tip of his finger, showed it to her and asked, 'What's on the menu?'

'Pumpkin soup.' She touched the place where he'd brushed her skin, as if reliving the moment. 'Pasta with a ham, cream and mushroom sauce. Salad. Chocolate mousse. Wine and coffee.'

'Sounds fabulous. Smells fabulous. My stomach's aching.' Other bits of him ached, too, and he thought she probably knew that. He didn't try to hide it. 'Where do the chopped herbs come in?'

'In the pasta. I thought we'd eat it all in the living room. I've lit the slow combustion stove in there, and it's already making lovely glowing coals.' She blushed, looking nervous and expectant at the same time. 'Which is a dead give-away of my intentions.'

'I love your intentions. I share them, one hundred per cent.'

They smiled at each other, and she reached around to close the door behind him. He captured her and kept her there, loving the soft give of her curves against his body, but she told him, her voice a little fluttery, 'Don't kiss me. I have to turn down the hotplate. Go and sit by the fire.'

'No, let me hang out in the kitchen with you. I'll pour us some wine. Can I stir something?'

Just me, Caroline thought. You can just stir me. But you've already done that.

He'd stirred her to depths she hadn't even had when she'd married Robert at twenty.

They stayed in the kitchen for as long as it took to drink half a glass of wine, then moved in front of the fire with their creamy orange soup in mugs. They still hadn't kissed. Somehow, they both seemed to know that once they did that, they wouldn't stop.

The expectation was intense, sizzling, almost scary, and Caroline felt it in every sense—in the flicker of the fire's heat on her skin, in the richness of the meal in her mouth. It would have been hard to set up a more encouraging atmosphere, but atmosphere wasn't always enough.

'You're really showing off with this mousse,' he told her.

They'd both lost track of time. Around eight, she thought, or a bit later. The fire had blazed down to a spreading mass of coals that glowed through the window of glass at the front of the stove. The fan flooded the fire's warmth through the whole house.

'Not showing off,' she answered. 'It's just more of those sinful intentions.'

'Yeah?' He smiled at her, waiting for her answer. Shifting closer on the carpet, he put down the wineglass that had been filled with mousse ten minutes ago and was now empty. He'd finished his coffee, too, and an hour ago, or more, he'd shed his tie, rolled up his shirt-sleeves and unbuttoned his collar. He looked rakish like this.

'I kept imagining the taste of the chocolate and coffee in your mouth,' she said, not taking her eyes from his for a second, trying to keep her voice steady. Seductive, even.

'Sweet heaven, Caroline,' he muttered.

Their mouths met moments later, impatient and giving and greedy all at the same time. There was no reason to stop, and they didn't. There was no reason to hurry either, but holding back was harder. The need and the intense response that Caroline had dammed back inside herself for weeks built like fire in a eucalyptus forest, volatile and explosive and impossible to control. Talk about fighting losing battles!

She'd never wanted a man like this before. She'd never been so aware of her own sensuality, so open about it, so comfortable with it. If it could only continue like this... They'd already turned the lights down low. The curtains were closed. The fire was their only witness.

'Sit up,' he murmured. 'Let me take this off.'

She knelt, sitting back on her heels and he peeled the soft angora up over her head, then reached round and unhooked her bra. She had a couple of frantic thoughts about her weight, then made herself let them go, flooding with heat when she saw his reaction to the sight of her breasts.

'Can I copy you?' she asked.

'Please.'

She unbuttoned his shirt, slid it from his shoulders, found a hard pattern of muscles like ripples on sand, and tiny brown nipples in a clean, even nest of hair. 'You're gorgeous,' she said. 'Tell me your exercise routine.'

'So are you. Gorgeously gorgeous. No exercise required.'

'Silly.'

'Very. Kiss me again, Caroline.'

'Your mouth?'

'Anywhere you want.'

Her nipples brushed his chest and he groaned. She ran her nails lightly down his back, then arched against him, inviting his mouth lower. They dragged themselves, somehow, out of the rest of their clothes, and the fire's radiance seared their skin to the point just before pleasure turned into pain.

They kissed and touched and explored each other, communicating everything they hadn't let themselves feel over the past few months. It seemed like a miracle to Caroline that he was actually here, looking at her like this, wanting her like this.

The guilty fantasies about him that she'd tried to repress couldn't begin to compare to the reality, the wonderful, frightening, unexpected reality.

She felt a familiar twist of self-doubt. Would it work? Was there any chance that it might build, and last? That he might *not* leave her hurt and broken at some point in the not very distant future? Maybe even tonight? Stilling her hands on his body, she brought them up to his face and cradled the barely perceptible roughness of his jaw on each side. He

had his eyes closed. It made him look vulnerable, but she didn't think he was.

'Declan?' she whispered.

'Mmm?' His dark lashes swept up, and the
incredible blue of his eyes confronted her.

'Can I tell you how long it is since I've done
this?'

'Is that an issue?'

'Since Robert. Ten years. Most of my adult
life.'

'You don't seem all that rusty at it to me.'

'I would be, with anyone but you.'

'I'm not understanding the problem here, in
that case, sweetheart, since it's me you're
with.'

'If I'm not good at it, in the end, will you
be—?'

He covered her mouth with his fingertips.
'I'm not even going to let you finish. Do you
think that "being good at it" is something you
achieve by yourself? I can't believe you think
that. It's chemistry, Caroline. Chemistry between one man and one woman.'

He began to kiss her, branding his warm lips
on her skin from the corner of her mouth to
her jaw, down her neck, across her collar-bone

to her breasts. The depth of sensation stung her, turned her inside out.

'Don't you think we've proved the chemistry's already there?' he finished.

Her uneven breath, almost a gasp, answered the question, but still she couldn't let it go. 'What if it disappears, before we—before I—?'

He stopped again, looked at her face again, turning her nerve-endings into an intricate web of lace with his hands at the same time. His words were almost a whisper. 'Are you saying you're afraid you won't reach your climax, sweetheart?'

She closed her eyes and nodded in silence, marvelling that he understood, and that he could put it into words.

'Is that what's happened in the past?'

'Too many times.' She added even more honestly, 'Most of the time.'

'And you think it was your fault?'

Robert hadn't ever said so, in those exact words, but she hadn't needed him to. Those sorts of unspoken emotional transactions could get so complicated in a less than ideal marriage. On the occasions when it had worked out right, when she'd managed to relax and push herself over that critical brink, Robert had been so obviously pleased with himself about it.

It was similar to the way he'd been pleased about having a son. He'd always, unconsciously, taken the credit. It could have been an endearing trait if her successes hadn't been so rare, if she hadn't felt such pressure.

'It doesn't matter whose fault it is,' she said, because she didn't want to over-simplify, or cast blame. 'It's disappointing. Both people get resentful after a while.'

Declan kissed her, soft and sweet, less urgent than before but just as delicious. His arms made two strong bands of warmth across her back.

'I tell you what,' he said, after a few moments. 'Let's make a promise. Let's agree that the top of the mountain isn't where we're aiming for right now. Promise you won't give another thought to that. We're on a different journey. Promise you'll just pick flowers all along the way and forget the top of the mountain's even there. I'll promise it too, OK?'

'OK,' she agreed, and laughed—a small, upside-down, uncertain kind of laugh because she couldn't see how it would happen. 'Forget it's there.'

'Forget it's there,' he agreed. 'You're not convinced, are you?'

'No.'

'Then I guess you're asking me to do all the hard work.' He exaggerated a sigh. 'Seems like sometimes a man's just gotta do what a man's gotta do.'

She couldn't help laughing at him, and when he grinned back, she knew he'd wanted her to.

'Let's watch the fire for a while,' Declan said.

He reached for pillows from the couch, and the blue velour beanbags that the children liked to lounge in. Sinking back to a half-recumbent position in the soft pile he'd made, he pulled her against him, cradling her back and shoulders with one arm and letting her knees bend over his thigh, so that both of them faced the fire.

For a few minutes, he didn't move at all, and neither did she. Truth be told, she felt sleepy. Is that what he intended? That they should simply fall asleep naked in each other's arms, blanketed in heat? He'd said they should watch the fire, but she found the flames too hypnotic, and just couldn't keep her eyes open. He was right. This was so nice, just this, no goals, no mountains to climb.

She was almost asleep by the time he began to touch her, and it was easy to obey his whispered command, 'Don't move. Don't wake up.'

'Mmm.'

'Or speak. You're not permitted to say a word, is that perfectly clear?'

'Mmm.' She laughed a sleepy laugh.

He stroked her nipples and pinched them lightly, then salved them with his tongue. For minutes on end, he traced the weight and fullness of her breasts with his hands and his mouth, and then he shifted position and went lower, leaving a trail of sensation across her skin.

Every muscle in her body turned to warm mush, and she felt so heavy that she half expected to sink through the floor. If he asked her to move, to caress his beautiful body the way he was caressing hers, she doubted she could do it.

But he wasn't asking, so that was all right.

His mouth trailed lower still. He supped her the way a bee supped nectar from an open flower, his tongue moving in soft, rhythmic strokes and circles, and while a part of her remained in a state of dreamy half-awareness, the rest of her body woke up with an electric intensity that made her shudder and twist.

Or she would have shuddered and twisted if he'd let her. Instead, he pulled away, pinned her hips with his hands, and let her suffer as he stroked the insides of her thighs, until she began reaching for him, grabbing him, silently begging him to come back. A moan broke from deep in her chest.

When he—at last!—deepened the intimacy of his mouth even further, she heard herself cry out in sheer relief, and suddenly there she was, on the top of the mountain, without ever having felt the labour of the climb. The view was spectacular.

'Oh, yes,' he said, as she eventually began to still. 'Oh, yes. That's nice.'

He slid away from her and she reached out for him, almost weeping. 'No! Declan!'

'More?'

'You now. Inside me. Please.'

She was so full and sensitised that his thrusts brought her right back to the place she'd just been, and he wasn't far behind her.

She kissed him feverishly as he shuddered against her, and somehow they were laughing, holding each other so tight they could hardly breathe, and just laughing.

'You totally tricked me into that!' she told him, her voice croaky in the aftermath of the moans she'd made. She felt so lazy in his arms. The fire would need another log to feed it soon. Not yet. She couldn't move just yet.

'I never did!' he answered. 'You tricked me.'

'How?'

'Ah, no, you didn't. We tricked each other maybe. Each of us took the other by surprise. I really thought there might just be the flowers, with the mountaintop saved for another day, but you responded so... Like a train, Caroline. Strong and unstoppable.'

'Greedy.'

'Didn't you notice what I thought about your greed? What my body thought?'

'Got a few clues.'

They lay there for a few minutes, while Caroline made up her mind that it actually would be possible for her to get up and put more wood on the fire. In the end, Declan beat her to it, and she watched him, enjoying the sight of a naked man with a log in his arms, and firelight flickering on his skin. Very primal.

The door of the stove squeaked as he shut it, then he turned to her and said, with an odd expression, 'We got a little carried away just then. I should have asked this before, but I'm not sure if I should ask it now.'

'Way ahead of you, McCulloch,' she answered, 'if you're talking about contraception.'

He looked relieved. 'I wondered, yes.'

'After what we said to each other on Monday night, I got an oral contraceptive prescription on Tuesday.' She couldn't help blushing. 'And the timing was right, so I could start taking it straight away.'

'Safe, then.'

He lowered himself to the nest of pillows and beanbags he'd built and took her in his arms once more. They watched the new log catching around the edges. Gold and blue flames crept silently along the splintered surfaces, and then a shower of sparks came as gas escaped from one of the half-burned logs and made it shatter.

Am I really safe? Caroline wondered.

Safe in his arms, yes, and safe from an un-planned pregnancy, but she knew there were other dangers. Feeling like this, there had to be. She'd thrown herself into what she felt, knowing it would make her vulnerable to his uncertain future here. She still didn't see how she could have acted differently, but what did she do next? Just wait for the axe to fall?

'This must be your regular time slot,' Declan said to Alison Scanlon.

He'd run into her twice in the supermarket on a Saturday morning, following the time he and Suzy had seen her. Since this was the clos-est thing he had to a regular time slot himself, he wasn't surprised. Both times, they had been cruising in opposite directions down crowded aisles, adding items to their trolleys, so they'd simply smiled and said a quick hello.

Today, however, he was later than usual, and he had Caroline with him, while Alison was just coming out with her trolley full of packed bags. All three of them stopped, and Alison said, 'It's nice to see you, Dr McCulloch.'

'You look great, Alison.'

'I've got a new job, at the Glen Aran Winery, giving tours and assisting in the tasting room, and I'm loving it.'

'Well, it obviously suits you.'

'Thank you. I never thought I'd be good at dealing with the public, and I almost didn't apply for the job, but after the cancer scare I just...' She stopped, thought for a moment, then continued, '...wasn't prepared to give in to my own faults so easily any more.'

'Alison, I don't know if you remember me,' Caroline said, 'but I'm the medical technician who was assisting Dr McCulloch the day you first came into the hospital.'

Alison smiled her new, more confident 'dealing with the public' smile. 'I thought you looked familiar,' she said.

'I heard about the great outcome you've had, and it really lifted my spirits.'

'Oh, thank you. That's nice of you.'

'It's a little selfish, too. I have a...a relative who's having cancer treatment at the moment. I need people like you!' She laughed.

Standing beside her, Declan could see she wished she hadn't spoken so frankly. She hadn't wanted to get upset, and foist her own worries about her sister-in-law on this near stranger. He said quickly and lightly, 'You're every doctor's favourite kind of patient, Alison. I know that's a terrible burden for you, but I'm afraid you're just going to have to live with it.'

Alison laughed and blushed and said awkwardly, 'I'm luckier than I deserve. Thank you again. I'd better get home and get my ice cream in the freezer.'

'Thanks, Declan,' Caroline said, after Alison had continued on her way.

She leaned against him and he captured her arm and laced his fingers through hers. 'Any time,' he answered. 'But what're you thanking me for?'

'You know. I dug myself into a hole just now. I might have burst into tears on her shoulder and started talking about Sandie in another few seconds. Alison's case has given me hope, and I've told Sandie a bit about it. Sandie got some encouragement from it, too, but I shouldn't have told Alison about any of that.'

'Blurs the professional boundaries?'

'That's happening too easily for me at the moment, and I'm not even talking about you and me!'

'Forget professional boundaries. You didn't put your foot in it nearly as much as you think. Let's talk about us. It's a subject I like.'

'Mmm, OK.'

'Us and our stomachs at the moment. We're shopping for brunch, but it'll be afternoon tea if we don't get to it soon. What do you fancy? Smoked salmon, cream cheese and capers on fresh-baked French bread? Or maybe—?'

'Stop right there. Don't waste your breath on any other options. It sounds wonderful.'

They had a perfect day, leading effortlessly into a perfect night. Very lazy, and totally focused on each other. On Sunday morning, they slept late again and ate another delicious brunch of sweet canteloupe and salty Parma ham that they'd also bought on Saturday. The sun shone into Caroline's enclosed porch-cum-dining-room, and Declan hadn't shaved, which gave him a wicked, rakish look that she loved.

'I was surprised,' he said, as they ate, 'to find you could buy prosciutto in this town. I thought Glenfallon might not get beyond white bread and processed cheese slices.'

'We have a big Italian community here,' Caroline answered, straight-faced. 'We've known about weird foreign food for a while.'

'Am I a spoiled, condescending Londoner, then?'

'A Londoner? You're not a Londoner! You don't really think of yourself as one, do you, Declan?'

Caroline heard the slightly timid, doubtful note in her voice, and quickly hid her face behind her coffee-mug. For some reason, she suddenly thought of the confident way Suzy Screenwriter had called him Dec, and knew she'd never be able to shorten his name that way herself. She didn't like the shortening, but that wasn't the point. Her own confidence was the subject at issue, and her apprehension about what lay ahead.

How long would he stay here? He'd already stayed long enough that he would hurt her badly when he left. How strongly did London pull on him? Would she dare to try and pull in the opposite direction?

'What do you have against London?' Declan asked.

He had a teasing look on his face, so she knew he'd missed the fear and uncertainty in her voice.

'I like Irish accents better,' she answered lightly, and was relieved to see him laugh and let it go.

They had a picnic in Carrawirra National Park and a hike up one of the marked trails, leading to a lookout on the summit of one of the highest hills in the low range. Declan whistled at the view. The day was clear, with only a light breeze blowing, and if the 360-degree vista wasn't postcard beautiful, it showed Australia's vast, unpopulated distances to stunning effect.

Crows cawed their descending, unmelodious scale, the air smelled of hot grass and no one had told the lizards that it was winter. They baked themselves on the warm, red-brown rocks regardless, and scuttled into crevices as soon as they were disturbed.

All of this must seem so alien to Declan, Caroline knew, although he didn't show it. She watched the way he climbed around the rocks in his nearly new hiking boots and khaki shorts, his bare legs and arms muscular and agile.

'What are you looking for?' she couldn't help asking.

'Spiders. More lizards. It's interesting.'

They ate their sandwich picnic in the shade of a eucalyptus tree, beside a small creek. Creek*bed*, to be more exact. The entire watercourse was almost dry, leaving just a few shrinking pools for the native animals to drink from.

'Wholesale meat and wool prices must go up when there's such a widespread drought,' Declan said, lying back in the shade.

'No, often they go down,' Caroline answered. 'Farmers eventually have to sell the stock they can't water or feed, and that creates a glut. They're vulnerable, because buyers know how desperate they are.'

'Right, I wasn't thinking.'

'It's new to you.'

'Fascinating, though. I'd like to learn more. It doesn't make sense to live somewhere so different and not come away richer for the experience.'

I could ask if he's made a decision on how long he'll stay, Caroline thought. Or I could hide my head in the sand a bit longer.

Hiding sounded good right now. Why spoil this?

She watched as he rolled onto his side and reached out for her, touching her face with curled fingers that made a tantalising caress. 'I suppose we should get out to the farm,' he said. 'It's nearly three.'

'That late? Then, yes, we should.'

She scrambled to her feet at once and began to pack up the picnic things, and they were on their way within a few minutes. In front of the gracious old homestead at Comden Reach, the dogs greeted Caroline with a detailed description, in the form of excited barks, about what a great weekend the boys had had.

And we're exhausted! two panting canine tongues suggested.

'Show us where everyone is,' Caroline told them, but just then Chris came around the house, past the water tanks.

'I've got the kettle on,' he said. They exchanged a brief hug, and he looked at Caroline's companion. 'Hello, Declan.' Like last time, his face telegraphed his uncertainty about the relationship. 'And I've made raisin scones,' he added quickly. 'Only they're more like rock cakes.'

'Sandie doesn't usually let you anywhere near the kitchen, Chris,' Caroline said.

He made a face as Caroline and Declan began following him round to the back veranda.

'She's feeling pretty crook today. Says it's just a cold.'

Caroline felt a twist of alarm inside her. 'But you don't think so?'

'Oh, I think it's a cold all right. I'm just worried about how she's going to fight it off. She's picked up even slower from this last cycle of treatment than from the first two, and I thought they knocked her out pretty thoroughly.'

'Is she in bed?'

'Only because I made her.'

Caroline and Declan looked at each other. They knew what an aggressive form of treatment Sandie was undergoing, and it could play havoc with her white blood cell count. Cancer treatment killed all the growing cells in the body, including disease-fighting white blood cells. She would need to have her next treatment postponed.

'Let me go and see her before we have tea,' Caroline said. 'Where are the boys?'

'Already getting into the scones, I think. Your Josh can eat these days.'

'He's growing, that's the trouble. I'll be out in a minute. I'll see if Sandie wants tea.'

Sandie lay motionless in her darkened bedroom, and Caroline paused in the doorway, thinking she might be asleep. But then she spoke. 'Come in, Caro. I'm awake. I heard the car.' She had a wad of tissues pressed to her face.

'Feeling rotten?'

Thanks to her treatment, she'd lost her hair, as well as more weight, and with this new ailment she really didn't look good.

'Disgusting. Even before this cold showed up, nasty thing.'

'Have you phoned your doctor?'

'Not yet.'

'He's going to want to admit you, Sandie, get you on antibiotics and have your next cycle postponed.'

'I don't want to postpone the next cycle. I want to get this over. I'm useless while I'm like this. Two weeks of nausea, followed by an Oscar-winning performance as a limp rag. A few days when the boys don't exhaust me within minutes, then it's off to Canberra for the next treatment.'

'They won't let you have the next cycle on schedule if they don't think you're fit for it,

Sandie. They don't want your white blood cell count to drop too low, especially with a virus.'

'And the worst thing is, it's not as if I can celebrate a cure at the end of this.'

'If you're showing no sign of diseased cells...'

'That's just the first step. I have to stay that way.'

'You will,' Caroline said, coming close enough to squeeze her hand. 'You'll eat well, and rest, and get fresh air and sunshine, and we'll all help. You have to keep your spirits up, because that's part of it, too.'

'Tell me something cheerful. I heard your Irish doctor's voice. Second visit, all this way. You seemed so comfortable with each other last time, too. Tell me that's good news. Did the woman in Sydney fizzle out?'

'Um, yes, about seven weeks ago. I— He didn't tell me until this week.'

'Why not?'

'Because he wanted to give this new thing a better chance, I think. He was right.' Could a voice blush? Caroline felt as if hers was. She could hear the rosy glow. Could Sandie? 'I'm glad about it now,' she went on, 'even though for a while I didn't know what was happening.

He pulled right back from the friendship you saw between us when we were here. It was confusing.'

'Lovely, Caroline. I'm so happy for you.'

'Be happy,' she agreed, 'but don't count on a future for it, Sandie.' Her voice wasn't quite steady. 'He's still planning on going back to London. He still has a job to return to there eighteen months from now.'

'Rotten career-oriented doctors, rotten cancer, rotten chemotherapy. I *want* to count on a future!'

'I know.' Caroline's voice fogged. 'So do I.' A future for Sandie, and a future for herself, with Declan. Warning Sandie against counting on that had only made her realise how much she wanted it. She'd jumped into this with both feet. 'Shall I bring you some tea?'

'Yes, please. Go easy on the milk. My stomach doesn't like much of it at the moment.'

'We won't stay long. We'll get the boys out of here so you can rest.'

'It's been great having Josh. Can you send him more often on the weekends? Mattie and Sam are a lot easier to handle when he's around.'

'I could keep Mattie and Sam, myself, instead.'

'No, because I miss them too much. It's so horrible. Wanting them, and then feeling too ill to be with them when they're here. Josh really helps. And it would be nice for you, too, wouldn't it?' she added gently.

More private time with Declan? Yes, it would.

'I'm glad my brother married you!' Caroline squeezed Sandie's hand again, and went to bring her tea. She had to pause for a few moments in the kitchen to make certain she had her emotions sufficiently under control to present a smiling face when she reached the veranda.

CHAPTER TEN

SANDIE spent the next three days in hospital in Glenfallon, and her next treatment cycle was postponed for two weeks. She received a blood transfusion to boost her white cell count, and was allowed home on Wednesday.

Saying goodbye to Caroline and the boys, she and Chris both insisted they wanted Josh to come for another weekend in ten days' time, as well as Mattie and Sam. When Caroline mentioned this to Declan the following Monday morning, during a quiet moment in the cyto techs' office, he said at once, 'Does that mean we can go away, just the two of us?'

Yes, please!

'To Sydney?' she asked.

'I'm sick of Sydney. Do you mind? Somewhere closer?' He bent his head towards her, speaking in a murmur, and his nearness wrapped her in familiar heat. 'I could wangle half of Friday afternoon off. Can we drive the boys out to the farm together, then head straight for Canberra or something?'

'You're offering to go all the way out to Comden Reach and back—again? With three hours to Canberra on top of that?'

'Only because I like the company.'

She melted, and said in a voice that almost shook, 'Canberra would be lovely.'

'Leave it to me. I'll book a motel.' He ran his fingers down her arm, and laced them briefly through hers. 'All you have to do is pack, and put in your best dress, which I'll look forward to the sight of very much.'

He stepped even closer, and would have kissed her if they hadn't heard Tom approaching at that moment. Caroline frankly wished her head of department a hundred miles away.

'Good news,' he said, pivoting through the open doorway, half a second after Declan had put himself at a respectable distance from her. 'Jaina Sharma is definitely coming to town this week to talk to us about the job and have a look at the town. You're available Friday, aren't you, Declan? To stay late, if necessary. We'll take her and her husband to dinner.'

'Friday night?' Declan asked. Reluctance showed in his voice, but Tom misread it, fortunately.

'Yes, you're right,' he said. 'Thursday night would be better, wouldn't it? They're arriving Thursday afternoon. And she can look over the hospital and the department on Friday morning. It probably won't go late, but just in case...'

'I'm available, Tom,' Declan answered.

He shot an apologetic look at Caroline, and she shrugged and nodded. By unspoken agreement, they hadn't yet been open about their new relationship in the department. She didn't mind. In fact, she felt safer, having it as a secret she could hug and hold, and the secrecy allowed her to live purely in the present for just a little longer.

With the end of her cancer treatment to look forward to, Sandie hungered for the future. Not knowing what the future would bring, Caroline wanted her own life to stay right where it was.

It didn't, of course.

That very night, plans threatened to go awry.

Josh, Mattie and Sam all looked at their dinner of spaghetti without any interest, and announced that they didn't feel well. They were up and awake, making emergency visits to the bathroom, for most of the night. Josh handled it manfully, but the younger boys needed help, and little Sam cried after every episode as Caroline attempted to clean him up. She got very little sleep and had a sinking feeling in her own stomach half an hour after breakfast.

She had a miserable day, but at least the boys caught up on lost sleep, so she had some privacy and peace. Could they possibly go out to the farm if this virus was still hanging round? she wondered. Sandie's immune system didn't need any imported school bugs to challenge it.

Declan phoned her at five in the afternoon, to ask, 'How are you, sweetheart? It's pretty lonely around this department without you.'

'I'm better,' she told him cautiously. 'Haven't vomited for two hours, and the boys have been feeling better since around dawn.'

'Sounds like a twenty-four-hour thing.'

'As a doctor, what's your verdict about how long we'll be infectious? I'm not taking the boys to Comden Reach if there's any risk to Sandie.'

'If you don't have any symptoms tomorrow and Thursday, I wouldn't worry.'

She crossed her fingers, waited out the two days, and began to relax. Josh, Mattie and Sam had all bounced back to full health and energy after that one listless day on Tuesday, and she'd sent them back to school and child-care with no qualms on Wednesday morning. No phone calls came from the school's front office, asking her to come and collect a sick boy, thank goodness.

Sandie wouldn't have reacted well to a quarantine, while for Caroline the weekend in Canberra loomed as bright as Christmas. She looked forward to it the way a child would, dwelling on it whenever her mind was free, seeing it painted in iridescent colours in her imagination. For selfish reasons, as well as generous ones, she'd have hated to cancel it.

With the boys' bags packed as well as her own, she picked them up from school at three on Friday, then drove to Declan's, where they would swap to his car. 'No insult intended towards your vehicle, Caroline,' he'd said, when they'd made the arrangement, 'but I'd rather spend the whole weekend in Canberra, not half of it waiting for road service on the Hume Highway.'

'I haven't had any trouble since that Friday in April.'

'Which means you're about due for some more.'

'Irish superstitious nonsense!'

'The theory works for my mother,' he'd said, then added with a grin, 'Occasionally.'

She'd given an exaggerated sigh. 'We'll go in your car.'

He was a little late arriving home. 'It would have looked rude to leave any earlier. Dr Sharma had a lot of questions. She seems serious about the job. Tom's overdoing his sales technique as usual.'

They got to Comden Reach at five, and Caroline was happy to see that Sandie looked much better than she had the previous week. 'I'm glad, after all, that they postponed the next cycle,' she said. 'I'll be able to eat for a week or two now, and put some of the weight back on, I hope.'

'You do feel too thin,' Caroline agreed, after they'd hugged.

'It's not a slimming method I'd wish on anyone!'

'You're sure you want all three of these monsters?'

'I can't get enough of them,' Sandie said. 'Every minute seems precious. Your Joshie's a good lad, Caro. You're going to miss him next year.'

'I'm already trying to save for air fares to go up for weekends whenever I can. I really respect Gail now for her attitude, and that's a plus.'

'Enjoy your weekend. Every second of it,' Sandie added slyly. 'Before dark and after.'

Declan and Caroline didn't reach Canberra until ten, having stopped on the way for a picnic supper of sandwiches and soup from a flask. Now that she was working part time, and would be for the next few months at least, Caroline had suggested the picnic to save money, and she was relieved when Declan seemed to enjoy it. He took things in his stride, she'd found. He wasn't pompous about his creature comforts, or averse to trying something new, and she liked that.

They checked into their motel in the up-market neighborhood of Manuka, then went out to supper at a café full of thin waiters and waitresses dressed in black, and groups of mostly twenty-somethings, talking earnestly about everything from politics to surfing. It was nice to be part of an urban crowd for a change.

Then they went to bed, which was still new, still wonderful, still a little frightening. New and wonderful to feel Declan's warm body spooned against her all night long, frightening to think of how much she'd already given to this. Her body, her honesty about what had and hadn't happened in the past with Robert.

Caroline knew that Declan could crush her heart between his hands without ever intending or wanting to. She'd given him that power when she'd fallen in love with him. She didn't know how she'd ever take it back if he left.

On Saturday, after a lazy breakfast, they toured the National Gallery and the War Memorial, and went up into the communications tower on Black Mountain, from which they could easily make out the swathes of burnt land left by the severe bushfires in the summer.

'You didn't pick a good year to see this country for the first time,' Caroline told Declan, with what was almost an apology in her voice.

She felt possessive about the landscape, protective about it. Every bit as bad as Tom, in fact, because it had become so important to her that Declan should be able to look at this place as a permanent home. She couldn't laugh it off any more, as she and Declan had both laughed off Tom's behaviour a few months ago.

'More than five hundred suburban houses burned in the space of a few hours. Hard to imagine now,' he said, looking out to the mountains in the west and not really answering her.

'Glenfallon's never been in much danger from fire, even in the worst conditions,' she said. 'The citrus groves and vines are kept too well watered with irrigation, and we don't have pine or eucalypt forests close to town.'

Oh, lord, I do sound exactly like Tom! she realised. Using every opportunity to sell, sell, sell.

'Want to go back to the motel?' Declan asked. 'It's only four, but I can think of plenty to do there before we go out to eat.'

Caroline could easily feel the desperation in the way she made love to him that afternoon. Just as Sandie was consciously storing up precious moments with her boys, in case the worst happened, she herself was staving off the future by making the present count as much as it possibly could.

Today she used her hands to pin Declan's wrists against the pillow above his head and explored his naked, utterly masculine body with her mouth. She drew a hissing breath of response from him as she sucked on the tiny buds of his nipples, and shudders as she ran her lips down the centre of his chest, and brushed her body in sinuous ripples over his.

She felt tears threatening to brim over, and grabbed for the sheet to wipe them away before he saw them. A few minutes later, he was so tender with her, his kisses like rain-soaked blossoms or berries falling on her skin, that she wondered if he had seen the depth of her emotion after all.

They showered together, lathering each other's skin with soap, and he aroused her with such an innocent air of not intending to do any such thing that she was laughing even while begging him, with the press of her body, to take her back to bed.

They arrived twenty minutes late at the restaurant they'd booked, and then stumbled into their seats in the dark two hours later to watch a nine-thirty movie, when the coming attractions had already begun. Leaving Canberra at twelve-thirty the next day, after an early lunch at the botanical gardens, Caroline wished she could roll back the clock and repeat the past forty hours over again, as many times as she wanted.

After picking up the boys from Comden Reach, they didn't get back to Glenfallon until almost seven, and it seemed sensible for Declan to come in with her and help put together a quick meal of eggs and bacon and grilled tomatoes and toast. They lit the slow combustion stove again, and even though, with the boys around, the evening didn't resemble their last one in front of the fire, it seemed just as precious, just as important.

'I don't want you to feel any obligation to stay on as long as we originally planned, Declan,' Tom told him.

It was a Friday morning, and the senior pathologist had summoned him just a few minutes ago to give him the news that Dr Sharma had accepted the employment offer made by the hospital, and would be ready to start work at the end of next month.

'You're speaking too hastily there, aren't you, Tom?' Declan suggested gently. 'Don't you want to keep your own options open?'

Caroline had told him of Tom's desire to take early retirement, but he knew Tom himself didn't want his feelings widely known just yet.

'Dr Sharma can't carry the whole workload on her own when you go,' he continued. 'Since I've come on board, we've got several more doctors in the region sending us their pathology when they used to send it elsewhere. Let's not risk losing that momentum.'

'Are you saying you're not in a hurry to leave?' Tom asked, narrowing his eyes.

'I'm not in a hurry, no,' Declan said cautiously. 'I have until the first of December next year to take up my old position in London again.'

He'd said this to Tom before, but this time it had a different ring to it in his own head. It sounded like the deadline on his relationship with Caroline, and he didn't like to think of it that way. He couldn't let things drift for that long, with nothing said. That had been such a large part of what had been wrong in his misguided yet oddly necessary affair with Suzy. There had been no structure to it. And structure wasn't always limiting. Sometimes it could free you.

His awareness snagged on that word 'necessary' that he'd just used in his mind. Why
on earth would he consider that Suzy had been
necessary? Because she'd brought him here?
Not really. He had the growing understanding
that she'd been necessary before Sydney had
ever entered the picture. She'd jolted him out
of certain assumptions, she'd stirred up his life,
and he knew the dust hadn't settled yet.

He'd have to tell Caroline what he wanted
very soon.

'Let me know when you've made a decision, then, Declan,' Tom said. 'Meanwhile, I
may put a few more feelers out. Dr Sharma
has encouraged me to think we may have a
chance at getting another pathologist to com-
mit to Glenfallon permanently, if we're patient.'

'I'll keep you posted. For now, I'm expecting a frozen section from Bren Forsythe, on a
breast tumour, and he'll want the result on that
as soon as possible.'

'Get to it, then. And we'll talk again when
we need to.'

On the way to the lab to prepare a section
of the biopsied material for the technicians to
freeze, Declan almost collided with Caroline,

who was returning from the department's bathroom. She looked tired today, and as if she wasn't feeling one hundred per cent. 'OK?' he asked.

'Not quite,' she answered.

She was making her usual drive out to the farm that afternoon. Declan himself was on call all weekend, so he couldn't offer to come with her, but he urged her, 'Take it easy, then. Could Chris come and get the boys?' He wished they weren't spending the weekend apart.

'I'll be all right. I'm finding it hard to get going in the mornings at the moment, but I perk up by lunchtime.'

He saw a frown crumple her brow, then clear again, but didn't have time to push her further on whether she really was all right. She never complained about the boys, or the driving. She'd reluctantly turned down his suggestions for last weekend, and had spent the entire time at Comden Reach, helping with whatever needed to be done. This week, she planned to do the same.

When he pushed her, as he'd done a couple of times over the past week or so, she admitted that she was overdoing it, but he knew he wouldn't get her to slow down until Sandie's remaining three cycles of treatment were finished. He'd picked up Thai food or pizza a couple of times and brought it to her place, to feed everyone and give her a break from cooking. No real private time—doing the dishes together didn't count—but he'd enjoyed the family time almost as much.

In the lab, he asked Irena, 'Is my breast biopsy here yet?'

'Just arrived a minute ago.'

Glancing back along the corridor, he saw that Caroline was heading for the bathroom once again.

'This isn't right,' Caroline said to her reflection.

She'd lost her breakfast in the sink about five minutes ago. Now she felt fine. This wasn't like the virus they'd all had three and a half weeks ago, when she'd felt achy and washed out for hours afterwards.

The virus.

The boys had had it in the night, but it hadn't hit her until after breakfast, when she'd already drunk her coffee and eaten her cereal and washed down her contraceptive pill, as usual, with a glass of fresh-squeezed orange juice. None of that had stayed down.

None of it. Including that tiny blue pill.

Surely...

She hadn't even thought about it at the time. She'd been too concerned with Sandie, and whether the boys would be contagious on the weekend. She'd been thinking about Canberra, too, anticipating in her imagination a weekend that had been every bit as good in reality.

Surely...

She'd been so outrageously fertile at twenty-one that missing her pill by less than half a day had given her Josh. At thirty-four and a half, she couldn't possibly still be that way, could she?

Could she?

She thought about how she'd felt the past few days. Queasy as soon as she got out of bed, struggling in the shower to keep her stomach where it belonged, craving a hot piece of dry toast. She'd had other symptoms, too, which she'd found good reasons for.

Fatigue. Couldn't that be explained by the extra work she'd taken on to help Sandie and Chris?

Sore breasts. Well, they'd received a fair bit of attention lately from Declan. They weren't used to it. She hugged her arms around herself for a moment and, yes, her nipples rebelled and her breasts ached. She thought about Declan, wished he was there and felt glad that he wasn't, both at the same time.

Sensitivity to smells. OK, what could she do with that one?

It stood out in her memory from when she'd been pregnant with Josh. Laundry detergent, tomato ketchup, toothpaste, dog food. Strong scents that she normally tolerated or even liked would ambush her out of nowhere and send her gasping for fresh air or a glass of water before nausea overtook her.

Cautiously, she squirted a generous blob of liquid pink soap into her palm from the dispenser above the basin. She brought it to her nose, inhaled and gagged, then had to take several deep, careful breaths out in the corridor before she could get her stomach under control.

Five minutes later, she told Natalia, 'I'm going to leave fifteen minutes early today, if you don't mind.' Their in-tray wasn't piled too deeply.

'Are you feeling all right?'

'Uh, no, I think I might have a bit of a bug.' Or a bit of a baby. Was it really possible? 'I'm going to stop in at the chemist before I pick up Sam.'

Self-conscious, although she didn't know the young woman behind the counter, she paid for a home pregnancy testing kit and dashed home. The new ones were so accurate. You could use them at any time of day, and the result only took a minute or two to appear.

And here it was, almost the same pinky-purple colour as the stainings she saw under the microscope every day.

Very pretty, and very, very positive.

Caroline had to collect Sam from child-care in ten minutes, and it was a five-minute drive. Picking up the telephone with her mind in a whirl, she keyed in Declan's office number but cut off the call at the first ring. She couldn't tell him yet. Not when they had no time to talk. Not when she hadn't thought through what this meant.

Grabbing car keys and bag, she set off to pick up Sam, her brain still churning.

How would Declan feel about her careless-ness? She should have remembered that a stomach upset could render the Pill ineffective for that month. She probably would have remembered if she hadn't had both Sandie's health and the weekend in Canberra to protect.

Thirteen years ago, Robert had been angry with her because the accidental pregnancy had disrupted their plans, even though they'd been married and had talked about having children eventually. She and Declan didn't even know if their futures lay in the same hemisphere.

Would he think she was trying to trap him with this baby? Would he think she'd done it on purpose? A pregnancy could be a potent weapon. Loving Declan, she knew he wasn't the kind of man who'd easily desert the mother of his unborn child, even if his motivation for staying was duty far more than love. Did she want to be the object of his sense of honour?

That, at least, was easy to answer.

She didn't.

She wanted love, honesty and a hundred per cent commitment, or nothing at all.

At child-care, Sam had paintings and collages to show her, but it was hard to inject sincerity into her voice when she told him, 'Mummy will love those. We'll take them to the farm this weekend to give her, shall we?'

They went home and had toasted sandwiches for lunch. The phone sat silently on the
desk in the corner of the sun-room. She could
ring Declan now. She could put Sam in front
of a video, and he'd sit there, happy and oblivious, while she and Declan talked.

But she still had to pack for the weekend.
She still had to come up with a plan for the
rest of her life, so that when she did tell him
her news, Declan would understand at once
that she didn't intend to make any demands or
any assumptions.

For the first time in an hour, her mind
slowed down enough to let other images come
to the surface. This wasn't just an unplanned
pregnancy. It was a baby, already growing inside her, already containing the tiny bud of its
future personality, waiting to blossom.

She remembered the euphoric three days
she'd spent in hospital after Josh's birth, and
what a miracle he'd seemed to be. Even Robert
had been awed, more emotional than she'd
seen him before or since. She remembered
how thrilled she'd been by Josh's first smile,
the first time he'd shown interest in a book and
the day he'd sat in his little bath and discovered splashing.

She'd had the usual difficult months of sleeplessness, the times when she'd felt like a failure because he wouldn't stop crying, the days when she hadn't even seemed able to finish a sentence, let alone the dishes or the vacuuming, because of catering to Josh's needs. Despite all of that, however, she'd loved having a baby and discovering herself as a mother. Simply remembering it, now, twelve years later, could flood her with a yearning sweetness she hadn't experienced since that time.

It didn't make sense, but already she wanted this baby.

She washed up the few lunch dishes she and Sam had created, thinking that he was playing in the spare bedroom with his cars, but when she went to look for him, she discovered him 'packing'. In other words, he was throwing dozens of random items into a canvas overnight bag, which she had to gently persuade him he didn't need for two nights at the farm.

By the time she'd undone the play packing and done the real packing, it was a quarter to three, and almost time to collect the big boys from school.

Declan and I can't possibly talk properly un-

til after the weekend, she realised. She didn't know whether this was a reprieve, an excuse or a life sentence.

Caroline and the boys arrived back from the farm at five on Sunday afternoon.

She'd managed to hide the tell-tale symptoms of her new pregnancy and had given Sandie and Chris some useful help, but she felt exhausted, and daunted by the need to prepare dinner and make a start on last week's dirty laundry. She'd have to hang the most urgent things in the lounge-room on a drying rack in front of the wood-burning stove, or Josh and Mattie wouldn't have school clothes for to-morrow.

She was still toiling to get a tuna and tomato spaghetti sauce prepared and a load of washing in the machine when the phone rang at a quarter to six.

'Are you back?' Declan said. 'Tell me if you're not, and I'll try again later.'

She had to laugh. 'Sorry, no, I'm not back. My body is, but the rest of me's still bumping along the dirt road between the farm and Cargoola.'

'That's what I meant.'

'Right. I thought there'd have to be some strange, nonsensical sort of logic in there somewhere.' This time, her laugh was more like a sob.

'You sound shattered.'

Yes, because, guess what, I'm pregnant!

'Could you come over?' she said aloud.

Oh, no, you're not going to lure him here and weep into his shoulder, are you, Caroline?

'I was going to ask that,' he said. 'May I come over?'

'Um, perhaps we should wait until tomorrow,' she revised.

Because I'm not going to be able to be strong about this today. I'm going to beg you not to go back to London, I know it, and that wouldn't be fair, even if you said yes.

'No, let me come over,' he said. 'All the more reason, if you're as tired as you sound. I wasn't called out and I had a very relaxing weekend.'

She couldn't answer.

'Caroline?'

'We should talk,' she said.

'When I get there?'

'Yes.'

'Is something wrong, sweetheart?'

Silence. Or at least, she hoped he couldn't hear how hard she was crying now. She had her fist pressed into her mouth, but her shoulders were shaking like a jackhammer. She had to stop this, because the boys might come in any second, starving as usual. The half-chopped onion on the cutting board might just fob them off, as long as this shaking stopped.

'I'm getting in the car this minute,' Declan said, because she still hadn't replied.

'OK.'

Deliberately, she left the ends and peel of the onion sitting on the cutting board as a decoy, because she knew her eyes would still be red when he got there. The boys were glued to the television, after a weekend spent mostly outdoors. They hadn't discovered her emotional state yet.

She hid her face in the steam that had begun to rise from the spaghetti sauce, thinking what a fool she'd been ever to consider Suzy Vaughan as the impediment to her feelings for Declan. Suzy had dropped out of his life, and that had seemed like a happy-ever-after when she herself had found out about it, but she understood now that she'd been focusing on all the wrong things.

She heard the doorbell ring, which meant he really must have got in his car the moment he'd put down the phone. Josh let him in. She heard the door close, and Declan's footsteps, and stayed hovering over her sauce, as if it might stick to the pan the second she put down the spoon.

'Hi,' he said behind her, and her stomach sank like a stone.

She turned. 'Sorry to drag you over here. Nothing's wrong. It was a tiring weekend, that's all. I'm still worried about Sandie.'

'Of course you are.' He took her in his arms and gave her a huge hug, and she could have stayed there forever, wrapped in safety and warmth and care. 'Want me to light the fire?' he asked, after a moment.

'Yes, then I can get dinner on the table. Will you stay once the boys are in bed?'

'Try getting me to leave.'

Fortunately, the boys were tired. She closed Mattie and Sam's door at eight, and Josh's at eight-thirty, and knew she was unlikely to hear a peep out of any of them until morning. They were all sound sleepers.

Declan was waiting for her by the fire when she came back to the lounge-room. He'd put music on the CD player and made them both some tea. Unfortunately, Caroline couldn't drink tea or coffee any more, because both drinks made her nauseous. She looked at the mug staying warm on the hearth and the man staying warm on the couch, and chose the man.

He held his arm ready to drop around her shoulders, and he was smiling as she nestled into him. 'Fast asleep?' he asked.

'Any minute.'

Caroline lay against him, listening to his heartbeat, trying to find a way to begin, and neither of them spoke for several minutes. She felt him kiss and nuzzle the top of her head, and her hand found the gap between his jeans and his shirt, and she slid her fingers across his skin, thinking that maybe touching him would give her the courage she still lacked, or the fluency to say what she wanted to say in the right way.

I'm keeping the baby. I'll welcome as much of your involvement as you want to give. I'm sorry to put you in this position. I was careless, but I'm not attempting manipulation, or pressure. I can't come to London with you. Robert would never let Josh go so far away, and I couldn't live half a world from my son. I know there are mothers who can do that... Maybe if he was a different kind of child, but he's not, and anyway I just don't think I could do it. I'll come as far as Sydney, if you want me to.

Preparing to spoil this quiet, lazy evening together with her roughly rehearsed speech was like preparing to leave a heated house and jump into an icy pond. She was terrified of how this could end up, terrified of all the wrong, impossible things Declan might say, and the more time that passed, the more impossible it seemed for her to tell him tonight.

Would it be so wrong if she didn't? If she waited just one more day?

Declan began to stroke her side. His hand nudged the side of her breast and his lips brushed her cheek. She turned to him, the helpless captive of his kiss, caught as always in the intricate net of sensation created in her by his warmth, his scent, his male strength against her.

'Better?' he whispered. 'Not so stressed now?'

'Much better,' she answered.

'Let's go to bed.'

CHAPTER ELEVEN

CAROLINE made love to Declan that night as if it were the last time, and believing that it well might be. She trembled as she took off her clothes beside the bed, and when he held her, skin to skin, a moment later.

'Cold?' he asked.

'Not any more.'

'That's right. That's how it is for me too, always.'

She slid on top of him, captured his face between her hands and gave him kisses like precious gifts, distinct and separate, as if she wanted him to remember every one. She kissed his mouth and his closed lids, his earlobes and the fine skin beneath, the pulse in his throat and the invisible line that arrowed from between the two wings of his collar-bone down to the hard, flat muscles of his stomach.

As she moved on him, she felt the new weight of her breasts and the electric sensitivity of her darkened nipples as a reminder of her pregnancy, but she just couldn't tell him about it and thus let go of this precious night, couldn't risk losing it when she might never have it again. She doubted he'd notice the way her body had already begun to change, despite how powerfully they were attuned to each other now.

And she was right. He didn't.

He laced his fingers behind her neck and lifted himself up, seeking her breasts with his mouth, then toppled her onto her side and took the dominant position, paying her back in kind for every delectable caress she'd inflicted on his skin. He could make her glory in her own body, purely because of the way he reacted to it, and she hungered for his body in a way she hadn't known was possible.

'Touch me,' she begged him raggedly. 'Don't stop. Any of it.'

Arching her back, she reached for him. His mouth was no longer enough. She wanted his weight on her, and she wanted him joined to her. As he thrust into her, she thought fleetingly of the life they'd already made together, rocked by their rhythm. Its heart should already have begun to beat.

But then all thought was swept aside as they cried out together, and only when she came back to earth did she discover that her cheeks were once more wet with tears. They fell asleep in each other's arms, and she only stirred when he left the bed in the early hours of the morning.

'Declan?' she said, her voice croaky with sleep.

'I didn't want to wake you. I'd better finish the night in my own bed. I'll see you at work.'

'Couldn't you get back to sleep after I left?' Declan asked Caroline the next morning, in the corridor outside her office.

She had blue smudges beneath her eyes and a papery look to her skin. He wondered, not for the first time, how he could take some of the load from her shoulders. Offer himself to her brother as a part-time stockman? Hardly! He'd had a growing sense, over the past couple of weeks, that fate had done a dirty trick in throwing the two of them together with such powerful chemistry.

On paper, they were no good to each other at all. Unless…

'No, that was fine,' she answered, cutting across his thoughts. 'I dropped off to sleep again straight away. But the boys decided to act like elephants this morning at around dawn.' She brought a fist to her mouth, and he thought she was stifling a yawn, but then she turned on her heel, gasped, 'Excuse me,' and raced for the bathroom, with the same urgency he'd seen in her, at a distance, on Friday.

A couple of disparate events and impressions threaded themselves together in his mind. Like coloured beads on a string, they began to make a pattern. He was a doctor after all.

Along in the lab, Julianne caught sight of him and called out, 'The Costanza biopsy is ready for you, Dr McCulloch. Remember? The case Dr Forsythe phoned you about yesterday.'

He knew it couldn't wait. A patient of Pete Croft's in the twelfth week of her pregnancy had showed signs of cervical cancer on a routine Pap smear. He needed to examine the biopsied material to determine if it was invasive. The future of the pregnancy would hinge on the result.

After an hour of meticulous scrutiny and several minutes of reeling off medical terminology into the microphone attached to his computer, Declan was ready to sign off on the

diagnosis. He phoned Bren Forsythe and sum-
marised what he'd found.

'It isn't invasive. It's CIN 2.'

'So the baby is safe and the mother will just
need a cone biopsy at ten weeks' post-partum.
That's good news. Thanks for giving us a diagnosis so fast.'

Caroline was back at her microscope when
Declan had finished his conversation with
Bren. He crossed the corridor and put a hand
on her shoulder, and she jumped. 'Ready for a
break?' he asked.

'I just took one, not long ago.'

'I noticed. You hared down the corridor,
like a teenager sneaking a smoke during school
recess. Again. Is that the second time today?
Or the third?'

This time, she flinched. 'Are you angry with
me?'

'Yes,' he said bluntly. 'Tell me if I
shouldn't be.'

Her voice dropped to a whisper, and he saw
tears brimming in her eyes. 'No, in fact, you
probably have every right to be,' she said, 'But
that doesn't mean I can take it right now. I'm
a bit of a mess.'

'Let's get out of here.' Out of the corner of his eye, Declan saw Natalia shift in her seat and stare at them. She looked alarmed, but he didn't care. 'Let's just go.'

He led Caroline to his car, aware of the careful way she was breathing, and then he just drove, not even thinking about where he was going until he realised he'd automatically taken the route that led towards Cargoola, and her brother's farm.

They weren't going that far today.

He remembered the sign for a picnic area that he'd noticed, in passing, on previous occasions. Just around this bend? Yes. He made the turn, and found a sealed road that led down to the river, ending at a parking area that was empty on a Monday morning. Caroline hadn't spoken a word.

She did so as soon as he switched off the engine. 'Have you guessed?' she said. 'You have, haven't you?'

'If you're pregnant, then, yes. I've guessed.' It came out more bluntly than he'd intended. She'd told him she wasn't strong enough for his anger today. Well, neither was he. Worse, he didn't fully know why he was angry. The emotion churned inside him, real and powerful all the same, and it rendered him helpless in a way he hated.

'I did the test on Friday,' she said.

'And you couldn't have told me that you suspected before that?'

'I didn't suspect before that. I put it down to fatigue and stress. Then I remembered that stomach upset. I did the test straight away.'

'And you didn't tell me. I had to work it out for myself. You didn't drink wine last night. You didn't touch your tea, or look as if the dinner you'd made had any appeal. I put it down to fatigue and stress, too, until I caught you running to the bathroom again just now, and remembered that you were doing it on Friday, too.'

She didn't answer.

He stared ahead through the car windscreen, then felt her hand on his thigh. The sensation of weight and warmth dragged his gaze in her direction, and he found a raised chin and eyes that glittered.

'Tell me why you're so angry, Declan.'

'I'm not saying it makes sense,' he said helplessly. 'I might even apologise for it in a minute. Possibly I'm being terribly unfair.'

'Don't apologise,' Caroline told him. Her jaw locked painfully over the words, because if she didn't clench her teeth like this her stomach would heave again. She opened the car door, needing the influx of fresh air. 'Just explain. You think I did this on purpose? Planned it in collusion with Tom, perhaps, to get you to stay? A baby's the last thing you want, obviously.'

She couldn't stand the confinement of the car any longer. Pivoting, she thrust her feet to the ground and stood up, then headed for a huge, smooth-trunked eucalypt that leaned toward the slow-flowing water. Touching its grey bark, she found comfort in the hard, sculpted surface, and her stomach settled back where it belonged.

Declan had followed her.

'No. A baby is not the last thing I want,' he answered, his voice harsh. 'It's not the last thing I want at all. It might have been the best thing in the world, if you'd let me in on the secret straight away. If you hadn't made love with me last night, knowing about it and saying nothing, leaving me out of the loop, for three whole days, on something this important. You know what that tells me? That you don't consider I'm involved. That you'll make whatever decisions you make without believing that my input counts.'

'No! That's not how I felt, Declan.'

'Then you need to explain. I don't want to be angry with you, Caroline.' He gave a wry, painful grin. 'Because I've discovered it hurts too much.'

Well, she knew how that felt!

'I wanted to tell you,' she said. 'I picked up the phone, Friday lunchtime, as soon as I'd seen the result. But you hadn't mentioned a future to this. For us. Tom told me just last week that you were still talking about your job in London. The date you had to be back there. I wanted to wait until I'd had time to think. I wanted to word it in exactly the right way so you wouldn't feel pressured.'

'Pressured?'

'There's nothing for you in Glenfallon. We've all known that all along. I've had to remind Tom of it more than once. The department's a waystation in your career. What we have…what we've had…is a waystation in your life. I realised that you would have assumed all along that the London deadline made that clear to me, and I felt blind and naïve for not looking that far ahead. Or not with my eyes open anyhow. Instead, I just closed them and fell completely in love with you in blissful disregard of any realistic considerations about your future or mine.'

'Caroline, you're wrong.' He stepped closer. 'About all of this.'

She let out a painful laugh. 'Is that possible? Think about what you're saying.'

'There's everything for me in Glenfallon. Tom…needs to be fobbed off sometimes. You know that. If we're having a baby, that slots the whole thing into place. The final piece that just fits it all together. I've been wanting something like this. Needing it. A truckload of cement.'

His accent turned the words into poetry, and her pulses began to race as her heart swelled.

'Something solid and real and unbending,' he went on, 'that I've never found before. I love you.' He took her in his arms and looked into her face, searching for the right answer from her.

'Oh, Declan…' She felt too overwhelmed to say more.

'That counts. So much. And we're having a baby together. That counts even more. London isn't important. It never was. It was just where I trained, and for a while after that there'd been no reason to move away. With my family scattered far and wide, nowhere else exerted a pull. Until now. You want to stay in Glenfallon, where your son is happy, near your parents and your brother and his family, and that's enough for me. More than enough. Because I love you and I want to marry you.'

'Yes, oh, yes.' Happiness flooded her, spilling as tears, turning into kisses, and they didn't say anything coherent to each other for quite some time.

When they did, it was about Josh.

'How will he feel?' Declan asked.

'He likes you.'

'As an unthreatening work colleague and friend of his mother's. How about as a stepfather? That's different.'

'Something for us to work on. I'm pretty confident about it, Declan.' She laughed, dizzy with happiness. 'Suddenly, I'm confident about a lot of things!'

'Like becoming a parent again?' he whispered, still holding her close. 'It's new for me, so you might need to help.'

'It'll be new for me, too, with you.'

'Tell me why you're confident about Josh.'

'Having Mattie and Sam with us and having Josh go out to the farm more often might help him with this, I think. Not to mention his half-sister and stepmother in Sydney. He already has a sense that families have blurred bound-aries. *Expanding* boundaries. There'll be some difficult moments, I'm sure, but nothing long term.'

'I'll do my best on that, Caroline.'

'Oh, Declan, I know you will! Robert said that if I married again, he'd rethink his insis-tence on Josh going to Woodside. Do you mind if I hold him to that?'

'Do I mind having Josh living with us, in-stead of bumping him off to boarding school in Sydney? Josh isn't the only one who's going to discover the joys of expanding family boundaries, you know.'

'No, I know.'

'You'll have a whole lot of new Irish rela-tives in your life when we take this little thing over to show off, in a year or so. I can't wait for that. So much I can't wait for, sweetheart, except I don't want to wish away any of this.'

He put his hand over her stomach, where their baby grew, and Caroline lifted her face and kissed him again, too happy to speak.

Declan did wish away some moments during the months that followed.

He could have done without the times when Caroline—first his fiancée, then his wife—was gripped by nausea, sleeplessness and backache. He could definitely have skipped that terrifying hour immediately before their wedding ceremony, when every doubt he'd ever had about himself in particular and the institution of marriage in general seemed to coalesce into an enormous, sticky, rock-hard wad in his throat.

Would he make her happy? Could he live up to the light he saw in her eyes when she looked at him? What kind of a father would he be, to Josh and to the baby due to be born at the end of March?

His doubts had disappeared the moment the ceremony began, and hadn't resurfaced in the months since. Caroline's parents ended their Queensland experiment and moved back to Glenfallon, to the house they'd once rented to him. They were already looking forward to taking care of the baby during the part-time hours Caroline planned to work. Sandie completed her remaining cycles of treatment and joyously reclaimed her place in the lives of her boys out at the farm. Christmas passed, with Josh away in Sydney with his father for two weeks. When he returned, Caroline moved awkwardly through a hot January, getting him ready for school.

Robert had accepted Ranleigh as a substitute for Woodside, and Declan's 'male influence' as a substitute for his own. Since they went out to Comden Reach every second weekend, Declan's apparently valuable masculinity received frequent shots in the arm. He'd learned to fix fences, administer treatments to sheep and drive a tractor, and was secretly astonished at how much he enjoyed helping Chris with the hard physical work of the farm.

Now, why was that? Just because it provided such an extreme contrast to his professional routine? More than that, he thought. It was about regaining a sense of family that he hadn't had since his siblings had scattered, years ago.

March arrived—the end of a summer that hadn't been nearly as harsh as last year's.

They'd had good enough rains last spring to fill up the tanks and dams and tide them through the heat. The sheep were healthy, and the garden around the Comden Reach homestead looked lush and filled with produce.

'This will be our last trip out here until after the baby's born,' Caroline said to him as they wandered around the vegetable garden together, picking vegetables and salad items for the evening meal.

'I'm looking forward to bringing my parents for a look at this place.'

'You're getting quite possessive about it, aren't you?'

'Possessive about a lot of things,' he answered, almost gruffly. He squeezed her shoulders and kissed her neck. Found it harder than ever to keep his hands off her now.

Sandie sat on the veranda, watching them, as they came back to the house. She'd put on some weight over the past three months after the frightening amount she'd lost last year, and her hair had grown back curlier and lighter than before. The whole family worked very hard on keeping her as well rested and healthy as possible, and so far her body was responding the way they all wanted.

'You've dropped,' she said to Caroline, as they came up the steps. 'Have you noticed?'

'I did think I was breathing a little easier today. And feeling sort of…' She didn't finish.

'I should think so!' Sandie exclaimed. 'Watching you walk just now, I could really see it. That baby is *low*!'

Declan felt a little impatient at Sandie for interrupting Caroline so quickly after that trailed-off sentence. Caroline was feeling 'sort of' what, exactly?

As he watched her covertly, she rubbed at her lower back and frowned. She was around three weeks shy of her due date now. She would be starting three months' leave from her part-time work in the pathology department at the end of next week, and people had begun to ask with annoying frequency whether they had everything ready for the birth, names picked out, hospital bag packed.

Josh had settled in well at Ranleigh over the past four weeks, just as he'd settled into the new family he was now a part of. Declan's parents were arriving next weekend for a two-month visit. When he'd announced to them that he and Caroline were getting married, and he was staying here, they'd told him, 'We thought about emigrating to Australia, years ago, when you were a baby. Isn't life odd, that you should end up there anyway?'

Odd, yes, but very good. Terrifying, sometimes.

Declan would have said that, yes, he was more than ready for the birth, impatient for it, in fact, but that didn't mean he liked the look on Caroline's face right now, or that thoughtful way she massaged her back with one hand.

'Everything OK?' he asked, taking the tomatoes from her so that she had both hands free. Hearing his tone, Sandie looked even more closely at the pair of them.

'Hmmm, having some interesting sensations,' Caroline said. 'Ouch. Bit more interesting than I want.'

'"Interesting" is not a medical word, Caroline.'

'It should be.' She began to breathe quickly, blowing the out-breath from rounded lips.

There followed another hour that Declan would have wished out of his life if he could. Caroline wasn't convinced that these were contractions. 'With Josh, I kept thinking they were, but they weren't, and then when they really started, oh, boy, did I know it!'

'Are you sure? Shouldn't we head back into town?' She'd had a quick and easy birth with Josh, she'd told him, but that was more than twelve years ago.

Sandie hovered anxiously in the background, wanting to help. Chris and the boys were still down at the river. If it hadn't been hot, Declan would have been sweating anyway.

'I'm sure they'll stop soon. It's not due for three weeks. I'm fine,' Caroline concluded. 'Let's get on with dinner. We'll eat early and...um...uh...head straight back...actually no, now this is one of the, oh, boy ones. Oh. Oh, dear. Oh.'

'What?'

'This is it,' she gasped. 'This is the real kind. I remember now.'

She leaned over the kitchen table, gripping it hard. Declan felt as if those white-knuckled hands were gripping his own guts. 'Let's go, then,' he said. 'Let's get Josh, and go.'

'I'm not sure...'

'You said you were! You just said—!'

'If an ambulance might be a better idea.'

'We'd be nearly to town by the time it could get here.'

'OK. Yes.' The contraction passed, and she breathed easier.

'I'll get Josh. Now.'

Declan hared out of the house. He trusted Sandie to take care of Caroline during the minutes he'd be gone. He met Chris and the boys on their way back, and gasped out an explanation, then turned back into the yard. Behind him, he heard Josh say in a strained voice, 'Is Mum OK, Dec?' and realised that he'd unwittingly frightened the stepson he cared about. Mastering his own jitters, he stopped in his tracks, waited for Josh to catch up and gave his shoulder a squeeze.

'She's fine, Josh,' he said. 'She's done this before, remember? And she was fine then, by all accounts.'

'Yeah, I'm pretty healthy.'

'I'm the one who needs a bucket of cold water. Over there, by the tap. Just chuck it in my face, OK?'

'You watch me! I will!'

'Good kid. Why don't you get yourself a quick snack, something you can eat in the car? Dinner might be late tonight.'

Back in the house, he found Sandie and Caroline in the spare bedroom.

'She's going to have it here,' Sandie said.

'No!'

Here? Over an hour from help, even at ambulance speed? No!

'But it's wonderful, Declan.' Sandie had tears in her eyes. 'I'll treasure forever that your baby was born here. So special, after all that's happened. A new life, starting here.'

'Here? No, it's too risky. What if—?'

'Stop arguing, you two,' Caroline gasped. 'Declan, I don't think it's a matter of choice!'

It wasn't. There was no time to do anything but have the baby here.

Their little boy was safely born thirty-five minutes later, and greeted at once with the name they'd already picked, James Gerard. Somehow, Declan gathered his wits enough to examine his new son and found him perfect— strong and healthy and ready to take the breast.

There'd be no need for an ambulance now. The only people heading out from town were Frank and Joy McLennan, impatient to see their fourth grandson. Before they arrived, Chris had managed to get dinner, with Josh's help, and Sandie already had bags of baby clothes and baby blankets on hand. She'd planned to give them to Caroline and Declan today in any case.

Darkness was falling when they heard the McLennans' car outside. Baby James slept in Caroline's arms, and she looked tired now, too. 'Funny the way things work out, isn't it?' she whispered to Declan.

'It is,' he told her solemnly. 'At the moment, it feels pretty nice.'

'Only pretty nice?' She smiled at him.

'You know how I feel. You know how perfect this is.'

'Oh, yes, Declan, I do,' she agreed, as he leaned to kiss her, his heart full and light with happiness.

With this woman, the mother of his new son, he'd found his place in the world, and he wanted to stay in it forever.

MEDICAL ROMANCE™

Large Print

Titles for the next six months…

December

IN DR DARLING'S CARE	Marion Lennox
A COURAGEOUS DOCTOR	Alison Roberts
THE BABY RESCUE	Jessica Matthews
THE CONSULTANT'S ACCIDENTAL BRIDE	Carol Marinelli

January

LIKE DOCTOR, LIKE SON	Josie Metcalfe
THE A&E CONSULTANT'S SECRET	Lilian Darcy
THE DOCTOR'S SPECIAL CHARM	Laura MacDonald
THE SPANISH CONSULTANT'S BABY	Kate Hardy

February

BUSHFIRE BRIDE	Marion Lennox
THE PREGNANT MIDWIFE	Fiona McArthur
RAPID RESPONSE	Jennifer Taylor
DOCTORS IN PARADISE	Meredith Webber

MILLS & BOON®

Live the emotion

1104 LP 2P P1 Medical

MEDICAL ROMANCE™

Large Print

March

THE BABY FROM NOWHERE	Caroline Anderson
THE PREGNANT REGISTRAR	Carol Marinelli
THE SURGEON'S MARRIAGE DEMAND	Maggie Kingsley
EMERGENCY MARRIAGE	Olivia Gates

April

DOCTOR AND PROTECTOR	Meredith Webber
DIAGNOSIS: AMNESIA	Lucy Clark
THE REGISTRAR'S CONVENIENT WIFE	Kate Hardy
THE SURGEON'S FAMILY WISH	Abigail Gordon

May

THE POLICE DOCTOR'S SECRET	Marion Lennox
THE RECOVERY ASSIGNMENT	Alison Roberts
ONE NIGHT IN EMERGENCY	Carol Marinelli
CARING FOR HIS BABIES	Lilian Darcy

MILLS & BOON®

Live the emotion

1104 LP 2P P2 Medical